I0527704

The Courts
Todd Bailey

Copyright © 2007 by Todd Bailey

This is a work of fiction. Names, Characters, places and incidents are the product of the author's imagination or are used fictitiously. Any resemblance to actual persons, living or dead or events is entirely coincidental.

All Rights Reserved. Published in the United States by LuLu
Enterprises, Inc., Morrisville, N.C.
www.LuLu.com

Printed in the United States of America

www.TheCourtsBook.com

ISBN# 978-0-6151-5420-6

Edited by:
Mark T. Bailey & Michelle Merschbach

First Edition
Cover photo courtesy of bigphoto.com

For my Family & Friends

THE COURTS

by Todd Bailey

I

The day was over ninety degrees and full of humidity. Sticky, muggy and just stifling. It had been an hour since McKenzie's best friend of the past 13 years had dropped him off. He sat on the ladder of his girlfriend's aboveground pool with his feet dangling. He had on a black T-Shirt and swimsuit. He was 18.

Her backyard was almost a half-acre of open space. Tall oak trees lined the perimeter. She was already in the pool in a one-piece suit. Splashing at him.

Take off your shirt.

No.

The backyard was prepped for her High School graduation party. There was a big tent and tables already out. The party wouldn't start for another two hours. Her parents had been out getting the last of the food and decorations.

When is your family coming?

My Grandparents should be here around 12:30 and my sister and her boyfriend are coming at 1:00.

She turned and swam away. She would turn 18 at the end of the summer. The party was going to be about 40 people or so. Italian. She was Italian, very much so. McKenzie would probably have skipped it if it weren't for the fact that some of her friends would be there. He had a bit of a crush on Devon. She was the Co-Captain of the cheerleading squad.

McKenzie got up on the ladder and did a cannonball while her back was to him. He caught her off guard and splashed the hell out of her.

Jesus Brad. What are you doing? You didn't even take off your shirt. He pulled off the drenched shirt and grabbed her as she turned. He pulled her close to him with a grin that he had carried for the past few months. Since they had gotten back together. She smiled and kissed him.

They knew that they only had this summer left. She was off to a state school and he was going four hours away to a Theatre Conservatory in Pittsburgh.

He backed her up to the side of the pool and she grabbed the back of his wet sandy hair. He slid the bottom of her suit to the side as she undid his trunks. She wrapped her legs around his waist.

Moments later she noticed her dad walking around the house. He was looking out at them, in the pool. Close together.

Hi dad, she said. The two of them stayed together and they pretended to horse around until he went inside.

That was close.

Yeah, she said. He knew that this might be the last time the two would ever be intimate or would even speak. Would he have had it any other way?

A breeze swept in and she got out of the pool. Her body dripped and she grabbed her towel as she was climbing out.

I'll go get changed and meet you back out here in a couple minutes.

OK. I'll wait 'till you get back.

She wrapped the towel chest high and walked toward the two-story home. Once she was in he got himself out of the pool and dried off. He stayed by the pool. Keeping some distance from him and the house until she returned. The two had dated seriously since they met in their sophomore year. By the time they graduated, the fights were so frequent that a split-up was inevitable. She dated one of his friends and he dated as much as possible. Making up for lost time. High school stuff.

McKenzie slouched in the white plastic lawn chair and sipped on a soda that was flat from the heat. Two girlfriends were at the table with him eating cake, dressed in late spring shorts and tanks.

The backyard had filled up and McKenzie knew no one. He thought, what shit to never have really been introduced to a single member of her extended family in over two years.

The way he sat, ate food, talked and even dressed was case in point for the exile. He knew it and actually took pride in it.

The two girls, Devon and Morgan, were actively engaging in meaningless, one-upping conversation. Talking about their summer plans before eventually turning to include him.

When are you leaving? Said Morgan.

Tonight.

Brad knew that the sooner he got out of the party, the sooner he could get on the road. Get a jump on the traffic.

That's cool.

Yeah.

Tim is coming to pick you up? Devon asked.

Yup.

There she is, said Morgan, looking over him.
McKenzie turned his head slightly to see her carrying a
plate of food and already talking at the girls. It would
be a long party if Pfifer didn't come soon. Over time
the three girls had grown into a clique that no longer
included him. He was OK with it by this point.

The hours melted on and he couldn't stop looking
at his watch. The heat. The conversation. One girl
going to Villanova in the fall, the other was going to a
state school. No common grounds with any of them.

I'm gonna take a walk babe, ok? He said.

Where you going?

WaWa. I gotta make a call.

Use your cell, she said.

I wasn't finished my sentence. I gotta pick up some
things for the trip. He got up and headed through the
tent toward the side driveway. He tucked his sweaty
hands into his pockets and raised his head. Heading
out he could see her mom coming from the house. She
was a typical, middle-aged *American Beauty* mom.

Short hair and thick-rimmed glasses. There was no alternate route other then right past her.

She felt the tension as much as he. She simply smiled, nodded and mouthed a hello at him. Surely, she did not want to rip into him again with ridicule. All of her guests would see her true colors. Surely she was afraid of him on this day. The two passed. He would not miss her.

As he hit the cracks in the sidewalk the temperature was no longer a bother. Maybe it was the personal freedom, the breeze of the walk. Escape.

The convenience store was a quarter mile out of the development. Immediately he pulled a smoke from his jean shorts and lit up.

The homes were late 60's to early 70's with a nice parcel of land. Mostly well-kept with blue-collar owners. The shade of the high, broad-leafed oaks was welcoming.

He broke out from the development and approached the main road. The shoulder allowed for just enough room to be comfortable. Eventually he got to the convenience store and crossed when traffic was clear. He tossed the butt on the ground and stomped it out with his GAP flip-flops.

Across town, Tim Pfifer finished loading up his '89 Jeep with a cooler, some camping gear and his suitcase. Tim's mom stepped out from the Levittowner and hung the last of her sheets under the driveway canopy. Her patience attracted calm. Sincere and subtle.

Be careful, OK? She said.

OK. I'll call you when I get in.

Thanks. Is Brad going with you?

Yes.

OK. Do his parents know? She said with no hesitation.

I'm sure they do. Why?

You know why.

The engine idled nicely. Some of the Jeep Green paint had chipped in the front but the mechanics were solid. Well-tuned for a two-hour drive. He did one last sweep around the vehicle and reassured his mother of his best friend's good faith.

We'll be all right mom. I love you. He kissed her and hugged her in front of the house. He took a last look at her and said goodbye. He got to the driver side door, climbed in and drove out into the street. Waving goodbye as he left, the cell phone in the center console rang. Halfway down the hill from his house he glassed the caller ID.

What's up? He said.

I'm standing out here at the WaWa. I gotta get outta here. I'm so done with this whole thing.

McKenzie knew that the sooner Tim drove in, that the sooner the next chapter would begin. He turned to look at the enormous warehouse across the street. Natural grass grew out of control near the entrance and along the walkway leading to it. Pale blue paint that had been rusted through on the siding heightened his vulnerability.

The Delaware River was a few miles down the road. Underneath the turnpike bridge, littered with garbage. Charred metal trashcans, burned out by homeless, lay strewn about. It's where it happened several weeks ago. Three guys from the worst section of town had raped a girl. One of them ended up shot and killed.

From what the Courier wrote the following week, the others fled the scene and left him to die. They found him four days later, under a mattress.

Last week he and Pfifer went out to see what they could find out. She was a good friend of his. There were no clues that they saw. It was all the news around. Like the time the class president couldn't even go to his graduation ceremony because of gang threats. This had been much worse though. It was true, a victim. Kelly Sanchez. That night, McKenzie held her. She sobbed uncontrollably. Bloody face. Her tank top was ripped. Her innocence, lost.

I'll be there in ten minutes. I just left. Pfifer hung up the cell and dropped it on the passenger seat. He sliced through traffic with the radio on full blast. He crushed through the gears shifting.

The wind was a way of life. He passed the High School on his way out to her house. A few cars in the parking lot. Probably just janitors and administration.

Gas was only two dollars and seventy nine cents a gallon in Pennsylvania. He pulled into the gas station, got out and headed inside. The young fellow at the counter looked up at him from behind the register.

He couldn't help but notice the foreign music playing, the Arabic written on the calendar and literature behind him, the overall rash of casualty that lay before him. He pulled his wallet from his khakis and got out some plastic.

Fill it up, regular.

OK. He said. Pump first.

He came to his car and backed out the gas gun. He laid it in the four by four and paced the lot. He could see the new football field across the street and down the field. New bleachers, astro-turf and stadium lights.

The board approved a huge budget that got the complex along with a new performing arts wing. The town was in an uproar about it, which brought some backlash on McKenzie, considering his old man was the President. It was a well needed change, but the tax increase hit hard on some of the lower-class sections.

In late November, the morning of the senior day football game, McKenzie was woken to find a rock the size of a watermelon lying in the back window of his dad's new Chrysler Sebring.

He always thought it was from a jealous boyfriend of one of the few girls he associated with during his breakup with Angie, or maybe someone he beat out for a position on the varsity team. So much in fact, that he roughed up a back-up cornerback in the locker room later that morning.

Looking back on it, truly it must have been an angry taxpayer. An election that might not go your way can bring out the worst in most people who vote.

It cost forty-seven dollars to fill up the Jeep with true unleaded. Pfifer headed back in and swung the door open. He paid the man, signed his receipt and walked out.

Todd Bailey

THE COURTS

II

There was always this sense of urgency in High School. Like, if I didn't get to do any of the classes or activities that were available to me then I would miss out on that path of my life. Nowadays, there is just so much out there. Clubs, sports, school government and even activism.

THE COURTS

It's so difficult for me to understand a Columbine or a Virginia Tech. Suicide has never crossed my brain. Trouble with me is that I came from a functional family. Our parents went to all of our practices and games, took us on vacations, made sure we had birthday parties and most importantly, always told us they loved us.

Did they spoil us with everything? Not exactly. They set limits on toys and TV time. My mom would always tell us to get out of the house and play outside. Now, whether she needed some peace and quiet is another story. Being a parent, I can certainly appreciate getting the rugrats out of the house to get some things done. Knowing what I know now, I can certainly comprehend the right of passage. I'll clean the whole first floor of the house. The kitchen, living room, dining room and anything else I can get a hold of and the kids will come in and destroy the place. That'll drive you mad.

Still, appreciating your children is not enough. You've gotta truly appreciate the moments. Tickling your daughter to utter laughter and tossing your son higher and higher each time. Making the best of the most unfortunate times and traveling. Show your kids as much as you can. When your teaching them what you know, in most cases you learn a bit more and the entire family grabs a bit more of life.

One night my son was already asleep in his crib and my wife and I were having our two and half year old daughter brush her teeth. She pulled her ladybug stool over into her bathroom. The cutest little stool, red and blue with big eyes and a half moon smile. One of the antennas had fallen off but she could care less. She scraped across the tile floor in front of the vanity and climbed up. We turned on the water for her and squeezed some Little Bear toothpaste on her Belle toothbrush.

That night she brushed exceptionally well. When she was done we filled a Dixie cup of cold water and began teaching her to rinse. We would tell her not to swallow the water and to spit it out. She would lean over the sink and mimic our actions. She spat but nothing came out. Still, she made a noise with her lips together, blowing out. The funniest thing, Teaching.

T he older McKenzie sat triumphant in the Widows Peak of SIO. The frat house was quiet as he sat with his roommate. They got to know each other over the past year. They perched high atop the countryside. They could see the peak of the dormitories on the horizon. Travis spit tobacco from the right side of his mouth into a cup. Liquor Control had been there just last night and shut down the whole scene. They talked and knew inside it was a good thing. They were just freshmen and it was all overwhelming.

What time are they coming in Mick? Travis said as he got up to raise the window and it's shade. The movement brought in a bit more air and revealed the four by four room. The writings in the sheetrock from former occupants gave way to the cracked caulk in the meetings of the walls. The smell of old dust, paint and spirit made the place feel as homely as his grandparents house from up state.

Around seven tonight or so, they should be here then.

Cool. You guys doing anything?

There's the Blues Festival tomorrow. I might take'em to that. You want to go? He looked out of the window to the entrance to the house. A rundown porch with an old couch parked on it. It must have been filled with dirt and such from the rain, weather and god knows what. We should get down.

Right, OK. Said Travis.

Mick lifted the hatch from the floor and Travis held it as he descended. They cautiously picked their way down the winding stairwell. Steps as close as a few inches.

They had to hold the wall with their hands because of the proximity and awkwardness.

They got to the main floor, opened the door and came out to an empty room. Across, there was a bar and the space looked as if it were the main dance floor to the top party fraternity at the school.

Travis headed behind the bar and opened the top drawer. He pulled out a vile, opened it and spread the powder across the tile. He proceeded to break it up. Did you want some?

No. I can't do that stuff. It'll bug me out.

Ya sure?

Yeah. Mick had been as straight as an arrow for the past three weeks. He'd been *randomly* drug tested three times in the past month.

Besides, I feel pretty good right now.

Travis ran the line and then made several sniffing noises to clear his nose of any excess debris. The two proceeded out of the 14-bedroom estate to the front porch past the mildewed couch and into the yard.

They approached Mick's red '91 Hyundai Excel hatchback with great care so as not to trip over any protruding roots from the ground.

They stepped in. The heat well over 100 degrees, no air-conditioning any more. They manually lowered the windows and rested their arms on the ledge. Travis adjusted the passenger side mirror to see his reflection. He checked his face, rubbed his nose some and swiped his mop top.

He pulled it out in reverse and the hatchback bounced over the uneven surface. She sounded like a go-cart or a battery powered child's car. The crack in the passenger side of the front windshield had spider webbed a bit more overnight to pass just under the rearview mirror. He pulled his right arm behind him and reversed straight down the driveway. At the bottom he skipped the curb and the two bounced in their seats. He pulled it back into drive and headed down the road.

Travis pulled the wad of tobacco from his lower lip and dropped it in the Styrofoam cup in the center holder. The LCB really took it to the seniors last night, hauling away three members including Charles "Chaps" Sanders, who was the frat's best president since Marvin Mittleton back in the late eighties. While Mittleton was known for his fearsome foursome nights which included all-night beer pong, no cover for ladies and topless chicken fights in the backyard pool, Chaps brought things to a new level, and last night was no disappointment until the shit went downhill.

They had planned the night for over a month with flyers, posters and even a myspace page dedicated to the actual event. On this particular evening, Chaps spread a plastic tarp nearly an eighth of a mile down the hill off to the east side of the estate. He ran two garden hoses all the way to the top to create the rapids and had splitters at several locations with various sprinklers. It was billed as, *"The All Night Slip & Slide Tournament"*, complete with a Jacuzzi for soaking afterwards. Perfect for nursing those injuries accrued coming down the hill awkwardly.

Admission was free for the ladies who were beating the evening heat in one piece, two-piece and less piece suits. The event had well over three hundred attendees, with all the local frats represented. Trophies were handed out and there is even a DVD already in production.

It must have been close to three in the morning when the LCB paid a surprise, unannounced visit to the house. There were roughly forty to fifty people still hanging around and the noise had died down considerably from the peak of the evening. Campfires ablaze and guitars strumming, it was actually quite chill.

Mick figured someone who had a bad run-in earlier, or was just out to cause some problems tipped off the right person, who in turn sent out the cops. They pulled him & Chaps straight out of the hot tub. They threw them both to the ground, and eventually hauled off Chaps and two other seniors charging them with the organization and distribution of alcohol.

It's down this way, right? Said Mick as he pulled the wheel to the right at the intersection of Main and Madison. I think it's up here on…

Right there.

Yeah.

He turned into the courthouse and headed into the furthermost lot. Unoccupied. The two got out and slammed the metal doors tightly. They crossed the street and up to the main entrance. As they swung the courthouse doors open Mick saw Chaps through the lobby.

He was standing in front of the clerk putting on his belt, holding a plastic bag that included shoelaces, some cash, keys, a lighter and some junk literature.

His grin was always calming and he appeared to even maintain his All-American good looks even after twelve hours in holding.

Hey guys, said Chaps. Thanks for coming.

Sure, no thing. Crazy night last night, huh?

Yeah. What happened after I left?

Everything broke up. We cleaned up a bit this morning. Since then, a couple calls from the brothers trying to see what the deal was. Other then that, you know. Travis was always one for summing things up. How about you, Mick? Chaps called out.

Mick was already entranced with some photos and awards in a clear cased shelf hanging eye level. Mostly old cop photos, PAL pictures, sponsorships and such.

Yeah, sure. I gotta meet my brother up on the exit off the freeway in about an hour or so. So, we gotta get going.

Right, gotcha. Chaps loaded up the rest of his gear and checked out with the girl behind the glass. The three of them promised to never have to step foot in this building again and stepped out into the late spring haze of night. Chaps seemed thrilled yet exhausted. They stepped down the stairs quickly and headed toward the lot.

THE COURTS

The night was thick and muggy. The courts were full. Older guys he didn't know. Some kids as young as fourteen years old. Out on a Friday night. Only one of the four towering metal halides was lit. It covered almost 75-foot candles. There were several cases of lager tucked behind Ramone's Dodge Ram 1500. He sat on the tailgate with Bob Vicente. The letters on the shoulder of his varsity jacket said RG and stretched his enormous bicep. Ramone twisted the cap off the bottle and shot it a good fifteen feet into the shrubbery.

There was a pick up game being played. Like five on five almost or close to it. Many of them were out of high school and were shirtless. The heat had started two nights ago and there was no end in site. Trailing sounds of cars raced by on the turnpike bridge just above them. The mosquitoes were out and lightning bugs blinked endlessly.

There were a group of sophomore and junior girls gathered by the bleachers sipping Bartles and James melon splash coolers. The most vocal of the group were Marie, Kelly and Daylene. The three of them had grown close the past year in the Drama Club. Kelly Sanchez student-directed a comedy with Marie and Daylene that won several awards at competition.

She wore high jean shorts with a black tank top. Her hair was cut even just above her shoulders and as dark as her shirt. She was slender in build with a complexion just a shade darker then pale. She drew the fruity cocktail up to her full lips and sipped quickly.

Pfifer sat at the top of the bleachers with one beer in his hand and the other on Devon's knee. He commentated the basketball game and entertained as usual. He was likeable to most everyone but had a week conscience when it came to respecting relationships. He had several fights with jealous boyfriends, rarely showed remorse and never thought he had done anything wrong.

I hate this place. McKenzie confided to Pfifer at almost a whisper.

Why?

Just bugs me out. Makes me uncomfortable.

Relax.

There's just no real reason for it. I never have fun when we come here. He got up and stepped down the bleachers. The apparent gloom struck his long face and left little room for healing. As he got to the ground he pulled Kelly's attention. Where you going? She said.

Nature calls. He did smile a bit.

Don't get lost out there.

He walked on the grass in front of the lot with his hands in his pockets. There were a few cars parked in the front row. Their exterior lights were on and he crossed the halogen beams swatting at the gnats and mosquitoes. He got in front of Ramone's truck and felt his throat swell up with anxiety. The two had never seen eye to eye since football season ended.

He wondered if the kid he roughed up was with him or coming any time soon. He wanted nothing more then to fly under the radar. Ramone was the star running back on the team and an all around good athlete. Not great, but good. The high school sports teams really never won but still there is that aura of the jock being the homecoming king, getting the girls and basically a free ride. He raised his head and acknowledged the lanky senior.

What are you looking at McKenzie? Ramone's thick eyebrows dipped just above his nose and he sat up in a territorial mode. Vicente smirked a bit and tossed a lit cigarette just in front of McKenzie. McKenzie laughed it off.

Just goin' to take a piss.

The girl's room is that way. Vicente laughed a bit more. He got to the edge of the woods and pulled some branches away to reveal a path. It was stark black and he held his hands out blindly.

McKenzie walked out of the woods and stepped into the paved parking lot. He rounded some of the cars all the while keeping an eye on Ramone. From the backside of the truck appeared a short and stocky body coming at him. His face was tight and he was shouting something about being out of school and nobody can stop us now. His fists were clenched and he was picking up pace. Now we'll see who the real man is, he shouted.

McKenzie dropped back and stumbled over his own feet. He caught his balance just in time to dodge the first punch and shoot in on his mid-section. He drove straight forward and dumped him on the pavement. The kid grabbed the back of McKenzie's shirt and ripped it up over his back as they fell. McKenzie's head thumped against the bumper of Morgan's Cabriolet and cut into his brow. The kid lay on his back with McKenzie squeezing him tight. He wrestled him over onto his stomach and locked him up in a reverse headlock. His knee drove straight into his spine and he pulled up a bit into a camel clutch. The kid's wind was already knocked out and McKenzie threatened him to leave him alone.

He held him down on the ground for about ten seconds screaming obscenities while Ramone and Vicente came over. Get up man, Ramone shouted.

I'm gonna let you up, but you got to leave me alone, OK? McKenzie released the kid's shaved head and abruptly rose to his feet. He stepped back a good ten feet not turning his back. Blood trickled down the right side of his face and the adrenaline was racing. His shirt was torn leaving only the collar and a sleeve. He ripped at it some more out of anger and turned to walk away.

The kid pulled himself up to his feet. Where are you going punk? He shouted.

Look, I don't want to fight.

Tough shit.

Just leave me alone.

Don't be such a pus'.

Whatever.

The kid came at him once again and McKenzie sensed his approach. He turned at the last minute. This time the kids' punch landed on his left temple. A flash of light followed with an immediate headache. He lost his vision as he fell back. The pain was minimal but enough to take notice. By this time a crowd of about ten others had gathered around laughing and cheering one or the other on.

Pfifer was walking across the courts with the girls. His face was filled with concern. Yo, knock it off. He shouted from a distance.

Fuck you Pfifer. Vicente said.

What's the point?

He's a smart-ass punk and deserves a good ass whooping.

He just let him up.

McKenzie dove at his feet but the kid sprawled out enough to remain on top and flailed at the back of his head and back. He tried kneeing at McKenzie but he was locked up too tight. He dropped his elbow into the center of his spine and the pain was great enough for him to let out a grunt. The kid was shouting about being from the tough side of town and that this is what you get. Pfifer dare not pull him off with Ramone and Vicente standing by. It turned into more of a wrestling match, the two of them rolling on the pavement.

McKenzie ended up on top again, this time he grabbed the back of his head. He pushed his cheek right into the street and the kid's nose dripped blood onto the ground. He did not throw a punch. He held him again for some time and eventually promised that he had had enough. He let him up and when he did the kid raised his hands as if he had just one a prizefight. He spit on the ground and they were both breathing heavily.

Pfifer shouted some nasty words at Ramone and the kid. Vicente returned the favor with propaganda. The two camps returned to their side of the courts. Angie came to his side and asked if he was all right. He was.

He pulled off the shredding of his shirt and walked bare-chested to the bleachers. He wiped the blood on the torn fabric and held it a bit over the small wound.

He grabbed a beer out of the cardboard case and sat on the first row.

He struggled to find his cigarettes and eventually lit one in his lips. He dropped his head into his hands and rested his elbows on his knees. He thought a moment about what had just happened. How dumb it was. How much he hated the kid for doing that.

The basketball game had dwindled down to just a few guys shooting random hoops at the near court. No real structure to it. They sat on the bleachers and Pfifer raised the volume on the boom box and it played Alt-Rock throughout the night.

You want to go back to my house? Angie asked.

Are you parents gone yet?

They should be gone by now.

OK.

Angie gathered her purse and put her sandals back on. I might be back, give me a call on my cell, she said to the other girls.

They walked under the enormous bridge and entered into her section. The streetlights cast shadows upon the pavement before them. They walked in the middle of the street only moving to the side for approaching cars.

At the end of Angie's street they stopped to see if her parents cars were in the driveway. They continued down the street and into her house. He went up to her bathroom and washed out the wound above his eye. It was just a big scratch and didn't need stitches.

The courts had emptied except for all but three guys shooting random hoops, the Drama girls and Pfifer on the bleachers. Ramone, Vicente and the kid drove away in the Ram 1500, spinning wheels as they screamed through the streets. They had killed a party ball between the three of them, their trash scattered throughout the parking lot and littered in the grass.

Real cool, said Morgan.

Some parents should not breed. Kelly sat writing her latest play in her journal, which rest on her lap.

Seriously. Marie got up and headed to the trashcan and threw out her half full wine cooler. I'm going to go to the WaWa. Anybody want to come?

Yeah, I'll go with you. Devon took a moment to peel herself away from Pfifer. He got up as well and they headed off the bleachers. You coming Kelly?

No, I'll wait here for Angie and Brad. So they know we didn't leave. Don't be gone long.

Are you sure? Pfifer locked his hand with Devon's and pulled her in close.

Yeah, I'm fine. She went to her writing as the three of them walked down the scarcely lit road. She looked back at the older guys shooting hoops. She took a moment to hear the silence. The sound of the basketball bouncing, and then plunking off the rim. Some light chatter and laughter from the crew.

She noticed three of them. Two black and one Hispanic or Puerto Rican. She gazed upon the courts and in a moment realized she was the only one left. The place had cleared out and she hadn't even noticed. She tried to swallow but her throat was dry. She felt her heart race a bit then she turned back to the court.

The hum of the light. She stared into it. There was a bang off of the backboard, which was in sync with a loud grunt. One of them had tried to dunk the ball and he hung on to the rim. She was startled and gasped. The sounds of the ball bouncing got louder and closer together until it stopped. The ball rolled off of the court and came to rest in the grass just in front of the bleachers.

Devon and Morgan sat on the brick steps off the front of the house sipping iced teas with mint. They sat with their backs to the door and had to turn when McKenzie's girlfriend came out.

Have you seen him yet? She said

No. Devon replied. He should've been back by now, right?

That's Brad for you. He's always one for suspense. She wiped the sweat away from her brow and pulled some loose strands of hair away from her face. Damn it's hot out today.

I know. Morgan got up and walked herself to the trash receptacles and threw out the plastic cup that had been beading with sweat. I'm gonna get going.

OK. Thanks for coming. I'll see you later ok?

Yes.

Bye, said Devon.

Morgan walked down the long driveway to her Cabriolet, got in and drove off with the top down. The two girls sat on the bricks and chatted about the past years events and such and eventually got to talking about what they would do in the summer and college.

A wind had picked up a bit and brought with it some scattered leaves and sticks that tossed around the yards. The sky had become overcast, which couldn't have come soon enough. Anything to cool everything off. A late spring shower would be nice. The warm rain hitting the face and washing the pollen away.

The air was thick and heavy. It had been several weeks since the incident at the courts and the oppressiveness just couldn't break. They trained their eyes and cheeks to shield out the penetration of humidity.

Many of her family had filtered out and most of the party was over except for the stragglers in the back. Two by two they came around the house and wished their best to her. Kissing both her cheeks, giving her a hug and then walking down the driveway. One by one, the cars gave way to open space.

Her father came out of the house in a loose tank top and shorts carrying a white plastic bag full of garbage. He approached the girls with slight hesitation. I'm proud of you girls you know. He said.

I know dad.

Thanks Mr. Saltucci. Devon wiped her hair over her shoulder and shot him a nineteen year-old smile.

Your parents must be excited for you Devon. Villanova is a great university and I'm sure you'll do great.

Yeah, they are. My dad is a St. Joe's grad so it's fun to talk about college with him. Where did you go Mr. Saltucci? She shot another adolescent glance trying to catch his eyes.

University of Pittsburgh.

Oh. Brad is going out to Pittsburgh.

Yeah. He pulled the trash bag along side of him and walked down the steps toward the large garbage cans. Yeah, I know.

He sat on the paved curb for the past half hour watching people go in and out of the convenience store. Wasting time between cigarettes and surfing the web on his cell phone. Oil stains a few feet from him in each parking space, some candy wrappers and butts lay just beneath him. He couldn't care anymore then he showed.

Steve Millers' *Fly Like an Eagle* played through the speakers above him. Very thin, considering the space that sucked up the sound waves. He sat with both knees almost level to his chest and his elbows stretched across them. He looked up again and across the lot toward the entrance from the main road. No one.

He pushed himself up and brushed the dirt from his shorts. He staggered through the parking lot and headed down the shoulder of the main road.

Overgrown shrubs and weeds lined the pavement and he kicked some pinecones and loose rocks as he walked.

Passing cars hit almost fifty miles an hour at that point of the road. The exhaust mixed with the humidity made for an awfully bad smell. He crossed the street, this time in front of the development. He ran quickly as the approaching truck appeared not to slow. One flip-flop got caught on the dirt at the edge of the pavement and forced him to the ground with some force.

He skimmed his knee on gravel and a bottle cap. Enough to put a nice size scrape on his knee and his right elbow wasn't in much better shape.

Dammit. He said in frustration. What a freakin' mess this is. He took a moment to lay on the ground without one flip-flop on and consider his place. He gathered himself and pushed up to one foot. He hopped to his flip-flop and eventually slipped the foot into it.

He shook his head and twisted toward the development. He limped slightly, putting his weight on his left foot. He pulled his cell phone out of his jean shorts, flipped it open and speed dialed. He raised it to his ear and paced on. The sun was gone. Hidden behind the overcast sky.

Boy, what a sore piece of crap I must look like, he thought. No answer. But that's just me, that's what I am. With this thought he galloped a bit and swung his scrawny elbows East and West through the air. He swiped his long dirty blonde hair back and skipped a bit. A smile came to his face and he knew everything would be all right.

There he is. Said Devon. She tilted her chin up and in his direction. Oh god, look at him. What is he doing? She let out a bit of a laugh with a huge smile. Mr. Saltucci turned from in front of the garage and saw him shuffle stepping several houses down the street. He pulled his hair and scratched his shoulder.

That better not be my son in law.

Could he be any more of a dork? She said.

Come on, that's funny. Devon stated. My god, is he bleeding? She laughed a bit more.

Oh god. She laughed now. Her lips raised into a slight grimace as she stood for a better view.

McKenzie thought, the only way to truly enjoy life is to be able to laugh at yourself. Laughter is a powerful medicine, he thought. His finale included a dim-witted pirouette and a grand bow. Devon did clap for him and Mr. Saltucci stared with a cock-eyed grin on one side of his face, under his thick mustache.

What happened to you? His girlfriend asked.

I tripped in the road in my flip-flops. Fell into the gravel and dirt. I scraped my elbow and my knee.

You want to use the bathroom? Grab some paper towels along the way. Mr. Saltucci said.

Thanks.

Here, I'll help you. She waved him along and they went in the front door. She held the front screen door open for him to go in first. He stepped in, careful not to get blood on the door.

The home smelled like your grandmothers house, and that's putting it nicely. That sweet smell of dust. That yellowish light. The wallpaper hung with floral patterns and the tough upholstery made it stale and uninviting. He treaded through to the stairs and carried himself as best as possible.

Go ahead up. I'll grab some paper towels and meet you up there. She headed through the living room and into the kitchen.

He passed the photos on the wall up the steps. Pictures of them. Pictures of her, growing up. None of him. Some of her dad running track and some of them on vacation at Disneyworld or something. At the top of the stairs was an old piece of furniture. A table of sorts. An antique. He had stumbled over it one of the nights in the past when he had snuck in at two or three in the morning. When everyone was sleeping, except her.

Candles were still lit in the bathroom and it smelled of potpourri cinnamon. The guest towels were out. He sat on the closed toilet lid and peered out the glass window that overlooked the backyard.

There were a handful of relatives remaining. Her mother was entertaining. How fake she is, he thought. Just the sight of her normally enraged him.

When the two of them wanted to go on a class ski trip the past winter with some friends, her mother had said no because they would be spending the night together in a cabin in Vermont and that didn't sit well with her. They all had a sit-down to discuss the trip. McKenzie, Angie and her parents.

They all sat idle in the living room. Separated by a polished wood coffee table. Her father in his leather EZ Chair, she sat on the love seat, Angie and Brad loafed on the long, hard couch. They were close together. An attempt to show some sort of maturity.

We don't think it is a good idea to let you two go to this cabin in Vermont, overnight, with your friends.

Come on, mom. Why not?

It's just not something we are comfortable with. We don't feel either of you are old enough to act as responsible adults. You're not even eighteen Angie.

You don't trust me.

It's not that we don't trust you.

Then why wouldn't you want me to go?

It's not the right thing to do.

Brad, what do your parents think about this? She dashed for the heart.

They're OK with it, I guess. He replied.

Bullshit. Mr. Saltucci sat up in his chair and ranted something to the effect of, "They don't even know a thing about it."

That's not true. Brad retreated.

I spoke to your father at the cast party of your last show and he had some interesting things to say about this ski trip. Mainly, that *you* are not even going. He said your grades were in the D's and lower and that your behavior was piss poor at home. His words, not mine. McKenzie rolled his eyes and slouched to the arm of the steel seat.

Whatever, I don't know what you're talking about.

I didn't think you would. The answer is NO. You're not going to Vermont on an overnight ski trip, period. He said. And that was the end of that.

Two weeks later Angie and Brad surprised her parents with an engagement ring.

McKenzie came to pick her up on the night of the Christmas formal and she wore a sleek black gown. You would think she was at least twenty-one. Brad insisted she wear the ring he gave to her when he picked her up. The tension was always high in the house, yet it was a bit silenced that night, considering the special occasion.

Her parents stood taking pictures next to her sister sitting on the love seat with her dull-ass boyfriend Michael. Eventually her sister chimed in with, "What's that ring you're wearing?" right before her mom snapped a picture.

Angie modeled the ring, mainly out of nervous energy and her mom took a snap shot. McKenzie keeps the magic moment in his shoebox as a bit of a keepsake. The look on Angie's face was priceless.

Teenage love is something of a paradox. Young kids think they know it all. But contrarily, life expectancy in the year 1900 was something around 47 years old. And before that, obviously less. Going down to 20 to 35 years old. The most important factor leading to our current extension in life, the advent of the modern day sewer system, which has stopped the common spread of disease.

From an animalistic point of view, 18 or 19 years old would have been a dominant age. While modern science has curved our expectancy to over 70 years of age our internal instincts have remained consistent.

She came up the stairs with the paper towels and cleaned his scrapes of blood and dirt. They came downstairs and back out front. Devon sat on the bricks talking to Pfifer. They looked up at Angie and Brad. His Jeep sat at the curb like a puppy waiting to go outside and run free.

Todd Bailey

THE COURTS

III

The Pennsylvania countryside along the turnpike takes you through the Appalachian Mountainside and into the heart of the state. A land rich in hope and morals yet lost or better yet, forgotten. A single room schoolhouse filled with Amish kids was disrupted when a 32-year old truck driver molested, assaulted and murdered 5 girls age seven to twelve in broad daylight. He carried a shotgun, a handgun and plastic ties to bind the arms and legs of the children. Horse and buggies stalled alongside the farmhouses have been transformed forever.

A mother's heart bleeds eternally with one unrelated incident. A father's dreams are crushed by cruel intentions of the mind. The soul of our Union paralyzed by a moment of time.

Outstretched limbs shaded the grass surrounding a single weeping willow in the center of open acres. From the horizon a crop duster dove just above the abandoned tractor. Hex signs decorated the barn and rancher while the rich brown wood peeled slightly from its seams.

All of the homes we passed looked the same from the outside, and as I traveled to the quaint town of Elizabethtown as a kid, I wondered about the families that lived in them. What did they do? How did they live? Where did they go to school? Occasionally, we would streak by a buggy or two.

I remember a little kid walking off the shoulder next to a carriage, same age as I was at the time. Like eight or so. He had farmer John's on and a straw hat.

His eyes met mine as I peered from the back of Mom and Pop's brown station wagon. That moment seemed to last forever. I wondered if he wanted to be normal. Well, at least what I considered to be.

We often loaded up the wagon and headed to "The Country" for weekends as kids. Dad drove and I sat on "the hump" in the middle in the back because I was the smallest and youngest. My sister usually gazed out the window and was pretty quiet. She was four years older then me and we never really had a thing in common until later in life, or so we thought.

For the most part I stuck to my older brother like glue. He was a year and a half older then me and I thought of him as everything I wanted to be. As kids, he always won. In everything he put his mind to. He captained the invitation-only traveling soccer team for Northeast Philly, made the all-star team in baseball every year he played and most importantly, was an All American collegiate wrestler, winning the Pan-Am games. He traveled to Cuba and Japan to wrestle and was the most sought-after High School athlete in the country.

Although I despised wrestling from day one, I went to practice with him, joined the teams and actually became pretty good at it, myself. He taught me a lot about competition. He showed me how to win with style and lose with grace. When he left for college, I felt so alone. I guess I should have been grown up by that point and been able to show how much I'd learned from him.

M cKenzie pulled his bare foot up and lay it on the dash. He leaned his head back and closed his eyes for a moment or two. He pulled his sandy hair back and rested his palms on the back of his head. Dave Matthews Bands' *Crash* played at maximum volume to drown out the wind.

As far as they were concerned the trip had just begun. The goodbyes he shared with Angie a few minutes ago were already gone. He pulled his lips up to a fine-spun smile. Pfifer lowered the radio as they approached the light across from the High School.

The light was red and the breeze had withdrawn. McKenzie looked three feet to his right and extended his arm as if he was going to touch the three-foot high retaining wall. The house they had driven past their entire lives had never been maintained. Hulking grass poured out of every crack, almost knee high at the most extreme points.

As they pulled through the intersection the music filled the Jeep again. The letters on the sign at the school read "Congrats Grads" underneath the school mascot, a tiger. Tim opened it up a bit on the mile drag through the closed school zone. He hopped the curb at the soccer field and drove straight toward the north goal post.

The tread on the four by four caught without a hitch and McKenzie grabbed the frame of the windshield for support.

Oh, shit man. Pfifer let out a howling sound and pushed it into third gear. They shot through the gold goal post and McKenzie couldn't help but lose his heart for a moment.

They pulled out of the field at high speed and jumped onto the pavement behind the elementary school. They rounded the playground and weaved in and out of the painted kickball and four man lines. Their faces were paralyzed with adrenaline as they rounded the school. The Jeep slowed as it approached the connecting section of homes.

One last stop before they hit the turnpike for the ride. Home. McKenzie wiped the sweat from his palms on his shorts. His face dropped as they crossed the main road on the cut through. They turned into his section, Indian Creek. One more turn. As they came down the hill, they slowed to a crawl with the music at a whisper. He pulled the emergency brake and all was silent.

They had taken too much time getting home. He could see his mother through the kitchen window. His dad's car was parked on the uneven driveway.

Across the street was a piteous home. So much junk spread out across the front and side yards that you couldn't help but look. Every neighborhood has got one and he happened to live across the street from the king of trash. Crap rats.

McKenzie's house was modest. Most certainly, it was the nicest on the block. His father replaced the siding with vinyl the year past. They had converted the garage and built a patio out front. Forty-year-old pine trees towered over the home on either side.

When they got to the front door the tension cleared. Funny thing is, as a teen, you may dread or fear talking to your parents but once you get closer you can anticipate safety. He swung the full glass door open and walked through the foyer. They came through the hallway to the living room.

Hey guys, said his dad. He was in throwaway clothes. Must've been working on the yard or another project. Mr. McKenzie was a gentle man who always wanted the best for his three children. For them to do even more then he. Not that he didn't take in all of life, he did. A State College graduate and high school teacher for over twenty years. He had coached all the major sports, was the President of the school board, a local politician and much more.

The McKenzie's had met in college, fell in love, married and were living the American Dream. Mrs. McKenzie dropped out of school her junior year to get married and later returned to school as a mother of three to earn her degree. A truly daunting task. Inspiring.

Brad's father took him, Mick and his sister to the graduation ceremony. He was young and sat in the bleachers as they went through the list of names. At the end everybody threw tennis balls in the air and Brad took one home with him.

They were as strict as they could be considering the unnatural control of adolescence. His older sister and brother were out of the house and it had been a tough year on him. A senior in high school, coming to terms with his own personal freedom and learning to take responsibility for himself. And it was even tougher on his mother. There had been too many arguments then he could remember. So much had been said and done. Her tears ripped through his heart. He was a disappointment.

McKenzie lived in the shadows of his older brother. He was little McKenzie with undesired expectations. They taught him that you are your own person and need to follow your own passions in this world. They did all the right things and he rebelled in spite. McKenzie had gotten a scholarship for his own accomplishments to an Acting Conservatory that he would attend in the fall. But it wasn't enough.

The fact that all of his friends had no real sense of family bothered him. The fact that his parents cared enraged him. He admired his friends as much as he admired his big brother and wanted more than anything to be dysfunctional. He tried his damndest to act out and tear things apart at their very seams.

The upright piano rest across the adjacent wall, strictly as a showpiece. No one played in the house. His mother wanted him to take lessons but he never did. When his parents were away for the night he would teach himself to play. Mostly just chords and tinkering around with sounds. McKenzie played the alto saxophone as a kid and could read music enough to get by. A few keys were dead or out of tune but he didn't mind.

Those nights, learning to play music and write songs were quiescent. He played so loud and sang anything that would come out. There were nights he would play so hard that he would ball over and cry. When he would go to school in the fall, piano would be a course and he liked that.

Hi Mr. McKenzie, said Pfifer.

You guys all set?

Yup. I think we are.

You got a full tank a gas?

Yeah. Just filled up.

Good. Brad, don't forget the box your mother made for your brother.

I know. I saw it by the door.

His mother came around the corner from the dining room. She was delightful. She noticed Pfifer.

Hello Tim.

Hi Mrs. McKenzie.

How are you?

Good.

Good. You guys will be back on Sunday?

Yes, that's the plan. Said McKenzie. We'll get in tonight. Check out the house. There's a Blues Festival were going to tomorrow and then we'll be back on Sunday.

OK. How was Angie's party?

It was good. He smirked a bit. Probably intentionally. Honestly, I said good-bye and I think I mean good-bye.

Oh yeah? She gleamed with joy. Why's that?

I think it's over. I mean, I'm ready for a new chapter in my life. This trip is going to change everything.

Well, have fun and be careful. His dad piped in. If you're drinking make sure you are not driving and try not to get in any trouble.

OK. We won't.

Can you straighten up your room a bit before you leave, please? His mom forced.

Yes.

Let me give you some money for the weekend. He pulled his clumpy wallet from on top of the piano and peeled it open. It was as if he had saved every piece of paper that was ever printed on. He pulled three twenty's from his pocket. Is this enough?

That's plenty Dad, thank you. He took the money and held it in his angular hand. As the boys walked back down the hallway his father turned on a circular saw that had been hidden behind the couch. The sound scared the boys and they jumped in shock. They turned and saw him bending down to cut a two by four.

They walked into his newly renovated bedroom, complete with Ikea furniture, 50's style Coca-Cola wallpaper and a waterbed. There were cups and plates with some uneaten food from the night before on top of his stereo system. His mirrored closet door was half open and some clothes lay on the floor.

He pushed most of the clothes into a bunch at the bottom of the closet and shut the sliding mirror.

I'll be right back. He stacked the plates and managed two glasses in his other hand and walked out of the room. Pfifer sat there at the computer checking his email. There were trophies on a shelf for his acting and directing. A small color TV rested on top of the dresser. He reached over and turned it on. He surfed to MTV and left it.

Over the reality TV programming and through the bedroom door he could hear muffled screaming coming from the kitchen. He looked down at his fingers on the keyboard for a moment. He focused his ears on the argument but couldn't make out a word.

As McKenzie opened the door he could hear Mrs. McKenzie shout.

And don't forget that when *you* go away to college.

OK mom. I hear you. He jerked back. He slammed the door enough to make the caricature print of him on his wall rock back and forth. Damn, he said. His eyes swelled a bit. He finished packing his gym bag with clothes and things for the weekend.

They stormed out of the room and McKenzie shouted, Bye, we're leaving. They paced though the front entrance way and leaped off of the concrete walkway. He jumped in the air off of the landscape timber and slapped the split white poplar trunk that arched over the house.

He threw his bag into the back seat and pulled himself into the passenger seat. He strapped his seatbelt while Pfifer got in. He circled the corner and climbed back up the hill. McKenzie collected himself in silence. He watched the passing homes on his street one last time.

You all right?

Yeah.

Levittown was sold as, *"The Most Perfectly Planned Community in America"* and when all was said and done, over 5500 acres had been developed in Lower Bucks County, PA with as many as seventeen thousand homes. The McKenzie's Levittown was truly the third of four communities built by Bill Levitt.

The Long Island Levittown built by Levitt and Sons in 1946, 1200 acres and a Government Defense Housing contract of 2200 units were both before the PA one and Willingboro followed shortly after with 11,000 units. By far the McKenzie's Levittown was his crowning achievement.

When US Steel's Fairless Works opened its doors, Levitt was ready. Mr. McKenzie had worked there for some time. Seen men die there. They felt a sense of pride being a part of something special, on a National level even.

The Jeep rolled by the historically categorized mirrored houses, no longer the same at glance. Half a decade had past. Critics said the houses all look the same and so are the people inside at one point. Nothing could be further from the truth.

The town had been scrutinized over the years. It was a high profile target for people looking to lynch the suburban way of life. 1979 was the countries first Gas Line Riots and it happened in his town, at *Five Points*.

Yet much has been made about the town and the concept to build a community including churches, schools and shopping centers and not just homes. Time magazine estimated that Levitt built 1 out every 8 homes owned by Americans in 1950. They then came back in 1998 and compared the settlement, "as much an achievement of cultural significance as Venice or Jerusalem".

The sun was setting over the Appalachian mountainside. The pink sun turned to colors of yellow and orange and resonated harmoniously with the tall landscape. The town was buzzing with energy. Summer was just weeks away. Most students stayed in the city to catch up on credits they had missed or just to lounge around. Maybe they would be going home for a few weekends to meet up at the Jersey Shore for some family time.

The sporting goods store that Mick's grandfather owned in Shamokin had been long gone, over thirty years. Lost were the days of coal. Still he traveled through the hills on several occasions. Desolate. The town had a sepia tone washed over it.

The boy's eyes spent no glance wastefully. Through the main drag they passed several college girls in their cars, walking the street shopping or goofing off. It was the time to make memories. The Older McKenzie soaked in all of the images, sights and sounds of college life. Travis sat in the back seat jittery. He could see him in the rear-view mirror. His bold oval eyes full of sorrow and low self esteem. Travis had spent the first two semesters of college in a constant haze of drugs, alcohol and depression. Rarely did he come out of the dorms other then to parade the street alone or hit the cafeteria on "freedom fries" night.

It came as no surprise when he received his dismissal letter. He shrugged it off with a binge marijuana evening and eventually got a local job at a telemarketing outfit and moved into an apartment. Things would never be the same.

Still, Mick was loyal to him. They went camping over the weekends and whisked their minds in creative thinking.

Chaps stared at his rough stubble cheeks and chin in the vanity. He pulled the skin from under his eyes and tugged at his dark full hair. I wonder who would have dropped the line to the cops last night, he said.

Probably Tommy Watson, little shit. Travis never liked the kid from Albany. He seemed to always go out of his way to bring him up in negative association. I seen him getting' bent with some of the brothers at the door around one o'clock.

Yeah, maybe. We'll never know though.

No, probably not. He conceded.

They pulled into a diagonal spot in front of The Smithson. The bar sat right on the corner of Main and Smithson Street and was the local spot to meet up. No one ever questioned your fake ID and they always had college prices on beer. Ten-cent wings, dollar drafts. They made it easy. Mick pulled up the emergency brake and yanked the keys out of the ignition. Travis already had one foot out the door.

I really appreciate what you did Mick, you know? He put his hand on his shoulder and sincerely squeezed it.

I know. No worries.

Travis pulled the heavy oak door open and the sounds poured onto the street. The jukebox was lit with Frank Sinatra at seven o'clock on a Friday night. The place was more then half full and the cigarette smoke had already begun to gather in the lights.

They grabbed a table just close enough to the pool tables and the big screen TV. They had an hour to kill. This was their table and this was their town. The NBA Finals pre-game had just started and there was lots of chatter whether James would get his first ring or not.

What do you think Mick? Chaps always included him in all of his conversations.

I don't know, we'll see I guess.

Pitcher of Lager? The waitress was Lynn, a sweet junior early education major. She worked at The

Smithson the entire past year and she always gave good attention to them when they patroned.

Yup, three glasses. Two shots of Jaeger, one SoCo and some mozzarella sticks too. She pulled her black hair behind her ears and smiled at him. Chaps threw his head back to the TV and Mick stood up.

I'll be back. He headed past the bar and into the restroom. From his pocket he pulled out his cell phone and dialed his little brother's number.

Hey, where you at? OK, that's like forty-five minutes out. I'll meet you on the exit ramp off the freeway. Exit 32. He flipped the phone down and tucked it away. He used the toilet and washed up at the sink. He sprayed his tie-dyed T-Shirt with water on accident. The paper towels were empty so he punched the hand dryer several times and placed himself directly in front of it.

Some people came in and out of the bathroom and he paid them no mind. He adjusted the shell necklace around his neck and took time to be certain that his teeth were clean. When he felt comfortable with his shirt he exited back to the main bar.

He sat back at the table and began to sip from the pint glass. They sat a while drinking beers and shots. Travis put another wad of tobacco in his lip and spit for a while. Several songs had played on the jukebox. Yuengling Lager was brewed in Pottsville, PA and is America's Oldest Brewery. In this area all you need ask for is a lager.

The walls of the bar were lined with Coal Miner photos from the area. An eclectic combination of oak and wrought iron filled the entire room. Air hockey and shuffleboard tables were always occupied and tonight was no exception.

Lynn pulled the fourth chair from under the table and sat with them. She had a break between serving her tables and lit a smoke.

That was a good time last night. It was a little too crazy for me with all the people but still fun.

She flicked her ashes in the ashtray almost continuously. She counted the money in her waitress book.

I had a good time too. Mick said.

What are you doing tonight? She said.

My brother is coming in for the weekend with a friend of his. How about you?

Travis and Chaps got up and walked to the pool tables. They had a loud conversation as they walked. It was loud enough for most of the bar to hear. Travis loved to try and get under his skin with trash talk. Chaps welcomed it.

No real plans. I'm off in a little bit. Not working tonight. You want to meet up?

Yeah, sure. That'd be great. At the house?

OK. Maybe I'll see if Jenn and anybody else wants to come out.

Nice. He's coming with another friend of ours that we've known our whole lives. So, it should be a good night.

Chaps sank a combo trick shot off the rail and let out a primal yelp as Travis turned away toward his beer. That's how it's done Travis. Concentration. He stalked the table and dropped to the felt with his forearm. What ever you do, don't take your mind or your eye off the ball. He looked up at Travis, pulled the stick back and then struck the cue with some power. The ball rolled the length of the table and sunk a stripe. That's all there is to it.

Chaps was more then the leader of the group. He exuded positive energy and that attracted everyone. You never heard a bad thing said about the kid. He was in his fourth year at school and not only managed high marks but also made good money as a young entrepreneur.

He designed and coded a local networking site specific to the college, fraternity and town that drew in some commerce through advertising and merchandise. He made enough money in the past two years to pay off all of his student loans. This, before he even graduated. Not bad for a part time gig.

Some people just have it. Whatever *it* is. If you are proactive, have the end-in-mind and always think win then you are most certainly guaranteed a higher success ratio. He could always be found with a self-help book or some type of traveling companion for positive reinforcement. And it shows, you can see the energy encompass positive people. And it produces for them. Chaps wasn't any different and future success was evident.

He ran the table and as the eight ball sank he pulled up and shot a crooked smile at Travis. Nice game. He bent over and shook his clammy hand. They grabbed their glasses, which needed refilling and walked back to the table. Mick sat staring at the pre-game analysis with a foot up on one of the chairs.

Uh oh. He caught Chaps' undertone. Another five bucks?

Whatever. Travis said. The tables at this place aren't even close to regulation. You know that.

I know Travis. Chaps grabbed the empty pitcher and headed toward the bar. Travis sat lowly and slumped his elbows on the table.

By now the tavern was full and the chatter was nothing more then white noise. The sunlight through each window had all but dissipated. Mick sat reasonably straight and was sure of one thing. The night had come.

THE COURTS

IV

As parents we often go the extra mile to create those perfect moments for our children. Taking them to the Philadelphia Zoo, the beach or even just the playground at the park. We set up these days by emptying our wallets as much as we can and packing up every possible thing that we can think of that our children will ask for or need. I like to have the lawn manicured and the car spotless and create perfection as best as I can, as if I am filming my own home movie and capturing these moments for them.

Truth of the matter is, children do not take note of streak free glass pane windows or the light jazz Compact Disc playing on the stereo. In fact, I drew my fondest child hold memories from quite the opposite.

My dad driving me to Lucas Lumber on a Saturday morning to pick up supplies for a weekend project. Five Satins playing on the radio. Picking up too much wood, so much that it would hang out the passenger side window and I would have to hold it down. The yard work you despised so much as a child suddenly becomes an hour in time that you would gladly give anything for to bring back, just to be with your father.

When all is said and done, the most elemental piece of this puzzle called life is family. Family can be your siblings, parents, extended family, guardian, or closest friends who have stuck with you throughout your time here on this planet.

Trouble is, the mind has a way of pushing itself away from all that we love. From the first day we breathe in air we are instinctively pushing ourselves towards independence. Determining where you fit in within your own connections or roots can guide you in a cleansing, spiritual awakening or it can set you back several steps by isolating you from all that may be good in your future self.

We spent our weekends at the Jersey shore. Growing up under the roof of two inner-city high school teachers wasn't by any stretch of the imagination luxurious. As a kid, I always thought we were rich, or at least more well off then my friends. Maybe my parents were just smarter in balancing their books. But most likely, it was their love that made me feel rich.

It seemed like an infinite amount of times that I walked the boards at Ocean City. Mack and Manco pizza. Dinners at the Crab Shack. Putting pickles in my eyes and olives in my ears and making the other people in the restaurant laugh. Embarrassing my parents enough that my dad drug me out into the parking lot and smacked my butt and punished me by giving my brother and sister my tickets for the rides.

That night I stayed at the hotel and cried while everyone else had fun. Good discipline.

We stayed at the Hannah Fin, which I had been told was replaced by condos but it hasn't. It still sits down from the lightning church on Tenth & Wesley. Its stark yellow siding and extended second floor patio. The sunburn. Soaking in a claw foot bathtub then being drenched in Aloe. I played miniature golf with my older brother and dad. We would wake up so early that the dew drenched my flip-flops. The double decker roof course was a favorite, mainly because of the anticipation of walking there all the way from 9th street. At the other end of the boardwalk was Wonderland. I could be there forever.

My dad would bury me in the sand. He taught me how to swim and not be afraid of the waves and even eventually body surf and long board. One night we walked the boardwalk and saw a guy on the beach flying a stunt kite, when they first really came out. It seemed like hundreds of people stopping to watch him and it was an amazing site to see. The wind pulled him halfway across the beach toward the pier. The kite twisted and turned.

The next day my dad went out and got us the biggest, baddest kite he could afford. We found some empty beach away from the main tourist drops and put it together. We spent hours flying the thing. The tension on the strings was powerful and I felt accomplished. He did that for me. Made me feel that. Eventually the kite came crashing down and hit a lone man and his dog that happened to be in the wrong spot at the wrong time.

I sat on the steps of our house one night talking with my parents about my goals in life. Seventeen years old. Talking about where I wanted to go to college and majors. The conversation erupted and I remember blubbering through my tears that the only thing I knew I didn't want to be was a teacher. I remember cutting through their hearts with these words, which I would take back if I could.

As a teen, you do things to get a rise. Still pushing the envelope of independence on the verge of manhood.

We had the lights turned out in our house once. One day I came home from school and the lights wouldn't go on, the TV didn't work. Nothing. For three days straight. So much that it spoiled all of our food. I was never really certain if we missed a bill or if we just didn't have any money. Looking back, it was probably the later. Raising three kids in the eighties on a Teacher's salary must have been the ultimate challenge.

My mom-mom and pop-pop lived in the same section as us, three roads down. My dad loved to take me there, then down to the creek at the end of the road. You never caught anything in the creek but you got to see some minnows and such.

The phone rang one night and I lay still in my bed watching some sitcom or something. After some time my mom called me to the living room to talk. Her eyes told me something bad had just come to pass. I walked out hoping I hadn't done something stupid again. I sat on the couch quietly with my arms on my thighs. I was reluctant to lift my eyes toward my father.

I heard the oddest sobbing sound. I looked up and he rested his head on my mothers shoulder, crying uncontrollably. His father had just passed on after a long battle with cancer, emphysema and mental illness. We sat in our living room for quite a long time talking about life, death and everything we could to get us through it. The words we spoke didn't mean a thing. It was the presence, the union of our selves and nothing more.

For a son, your father is everything. An irreplaceable heirloom passed on for generations. A swelling wave approaching off the horizon. An unforgettable moment in time. This loss is an endless pit.

The wind pounded his open palm as he rested it outside the Jeep. He flipped it horizontally to cut through the air and swayed it up and down like he was the wing of an airplane. Keeping it steady was difficult at this speed. The road cut right through the mountainside and his ears popped. Signs for *Falling Rocks* passed every other mile or so. *"The World's Most Scenic Highway"* runs 359 miles from the Delaware River to Ohio and will run you just under $20.00 to make the full ride.

Eighty miles out from Lebanon the boys exited into a rest stop. The Jeep steadily decreased in speed and McKenzie pulled his leg down from the dash. He tossed the remains of the lit cigarette out of the window and dropped his sunglasses back over his eyes. The butt bounced along the road and finally came to rest next to the abandoned tire shredding and trash on the shoulder. He reached over into the backseat and zipped his gym bag. He rounded up the empty water bottles and soda bottles.

They pulled into the lot outside the complex and parked at the first spot they saw. No stalking or cruising for a front row spot. Just park, get out and walk. He threw out the bottles on his way in. Pfifer adjusted his collar and walked with a bounce toward the entrance. Wind was calm. Many people going in and out at a quick pace. Actual confusion. Inside there was an abundance of choices for retail. Gift shops, restaurants, and an arcade. Pfifer spotted the restroom and they headed that way. They bumped shoulders with several people as they shuffled through the crowd. Amazing, the amount of people there were.

McKenzie headed into a stall and closed the door. He sat for a moment. Tags and incoherent scribbles on the inside of the bathroom stall. He looked at them all. Questioning each of their origin. Someone at sometime actually took the time to deface the walls. Somebody was actually that stupid. He checked his messages on his cell phone.

I'll meet you out at the Jeep, alright? He heard Pfifer say with a deep echo in the long tiled room.

OK. A vulnerable state.

Pfifer paced through until he was drawn to a charity box that sat on a countertop near a sunglass vendor. It was unoccupied. He stopped a moment and hid himself in the shuffle of the passing crowd. Watched it for a moment, then darted toward it. He quickly picked it up and held it to his chest. He made his way straight out the front door maintaining his composure.

He broke out into the dusky night with the plastic case tucked away. Once outside he walked off the path and ducked through some foliage. He got to the Jeep and threw it under an afghan blanket in the back seat. He climbed in and started up the Jeep. By the time he reversed out of the spot McKenzie was there.

C'mon. He waved him to pick it up. He kept walking and drew a blank stare. No sooner then the time he got in the seat Pfifer floored it.

What are you doing?

Hold on a second. He was smiling and McKenzie new something happened. What is it?

Take a look in the back seat. Under the blanket. He turned around and pulled it up. Jesus Christ. Oh my god. What did you do?

I just seen it. Check it out. See how much is in there.

He sat it on his lap and read the letter on top. You are an evil man. He said to Pfifer. It was a homemade letter printed off a desktop and had a photo of a little girl on it. She was mostly bald and very cute. *Please kindly donate your loose change and support our daughter Kayla Marie Sanderson who is battling Childhood Leukemia.* There was a logo of St. Jude's Hospital.

Damn you Tim. You are a sick kid.

Oh, come on man. It's no different then ripping off the Ronald McDonald Fund boxes at the drive thru windows.

Yes, it is. This is personal. Someone's daughter. A family is trying to collect money to pay off hospital bills. That's awful man.

Relax. He yielded onto the turnpike and pulled it up to 85 mph. The sound of the wind picked up and he slapped on Vitalogy, which would take them all the way there. Eventually, they both laughed it off and McKenzie pulled out the cash and counted out 64 dollars and some change. He tossed the case out of the Jeep when the road was clear. They agreed to split the money, still it left a pitting feeling in McKenzie's stomach.

Several miles up the road they pulled off the turnpike and drove to a warehouse sized fireworks store. Wal-Mart sized aisles filled with anything imaginable. They scraped together the charity money and loaded up with two big brown bags full of high-powered bangers.

It was almost eight o'clock at night and they had already been at the exit a good fifteen minutes. Travis got out to take a walk into the woods and pee. He stumbled off the road and disappeared behind the trees. Mick changed the radio stations as if he were tuning in for aliens.

Could you please just leave one station on? Said
Chaps.

He left on white noise and sat back and crossed his
eyes at him. Chaps reached down and turned it off.
The sound of the engine. A tap on the driver's side
window made them both jump.

Standing tall and shaded was a state trooper with
his flashlight in hand. He flipped his hand in a gesture
to roll down the window. Mick mouthed the words oh
shit. He looked at the cop and rolled the dirty window
down as far as it could go.

Hi.

License, insurance, registration. He reached over
Chaps to the glove box and pulled it out. The entire
compartment fell out of the dash to the floor. Papers
spread out everywhere. He pulled a vinyl pouch from
them and began sorting through it.

What are you guys doing out here?

Were waiting for my brother to come off the
turnpike. He's running a bit late, should be here any
minute though.

Where's your friend gone off to?

What?

The kid that went in the woods.

Oh. Ummm… I think this is my registration. He handed it over.

This is expired.

OK, it's this one then. He handed him another card with his insurance. I don't know where he went off to. He said he'd be right back.

Your license?

He reached in his pocket and pulled out his wallet. Here you go.

You two sit tight, ok?

A second officer was already at the edge of the woods flashing his light and calling out to Travis. The first officer turned to him. You see him?

Yeah, he's coming.

OK, I'm gonna run this right quick. He went back to his patrol car. Travis appeared from the woods with his shorts half on. The officer took him to the back of the Excel and had him sit on the bumper.

McKenzie spotted the spinning lights from the tollbooth. Oh my god. That's them with the cops.

Pfifer paid the $6.40 toll and slowly pulled out. What should I do?

Shit, man. Pull up behind them.

Are you sure?

Yeah, we'll be alright. He put his flashers on and stopped the Jeep some fifteen feet behind the cars. He put it in park and they sat there on the countryside road. Who's that guy sitting on the car?

I have no clue, said McKenzie.

What do you think happened?

This is not good man. I'm gonna go out there.

No, just wait.

The officer questioned Travis, who's in the Jeep?

That's probably Mick's brother. We've been waiting for him. He's not from around here and doesn't know the area very well.

Time stood still and it seemed like hours before the other officer appeared again. He pulled himself up from the Crown Victoria and put his brimmed hat on carefully. He rest one hand on his piece and walked sternly.

Would you mind stepping out of the vehicle please?

Can I ask what for?

Step out of the vehicle.

Mick pulled the handle and the door squealed open.

Come around to the front of the vehicle please. He pointed toward the front and created some space. How much have you had to drink tonight?

Not much, maybe two beers.

Two beers? That's it?

Yeah.

I smelled the alcohol as soon as I walked up to your vehicle. This may be your only chance to come clean on this. So, I'll give you another opportunity to be honest with me, which could help you in the future. Do you understand what I am saying to you?

Yes sir.

How much have you had to drink tonight?

Two beers and maybe a shot.

A shot of what?

Southern Comfort.

I have reason to think that you may be under the influence and I'm going to need to check your levels and conduct a field sobriety test. Are you OK with that?

Do I have any choice?

Well, you can decline and then I would take you down to the police station and this would be an all night thing.

OK.

What I'm going to ask you to do is repeat the same motions I do. The officer went on to point to his nose with one hand. He had him walk a line and do the alphabet.

Son, I do not know that I am confident that you have passed these field tests and am going to have to ask you to blow in to this apparatus so I can get an accurate reading on your alcohol level. He put it up to Mick's mouth. Please blow. Harder.

Mick closed his eyes and blew strongly into the straw.

Now wait here with your hands firmly placed on the hood. The officer walked away and Mick noticed the Jeep.

He caught eyes with the boys. Brad looked at him deeply as if to say what's going on. Mick shrugged I don't know.

The other officer questioned Travis about his identification and what he was doing in the woods. After some time, he wrote him a citation for seventy-two dollars and told him to be more respectful when nature calls.

The cop sat in his car punching keys at the mounted computer on the dashboard. He took several minutes then pulled himself back out of the car and approached McKenzie.

You should not be driving this vehicle right now. Your level is just below the legal limit at point zero seven. I'm going to let you off with a warning right now but one of your pals is going to have to drive. I know who you are too. You had a great season this past year and you need to be more careful. Maybe you aren't hanging around the right crowd. You're a good kid and you have a bright future. I've seen it too many times with star athletes here. Don't throw it away.

He handed his documents over to him and walked toward Chaps window. Are you all right to drive home?

Yes sir.

Let's make it happen, your buddy is getting off with a warning tonight but I don't want to see you guys again, understand?

Yes sir.

Mick walked to the Jeep. What happened? Let's talk about it at the house. Follow us, ok? He walked back to the Excel and they drove off. Travis sat in the back screaming up a storm over the ticket. Chaps drove cautiously through the winding single lane road. Farmhouses tucked off the shoulder an eighth of a mile. McKenzie sat staring out the window.

What he say to you? Chaps probed.

He said I blew a .07 and that I should be more careful. Said he new who I was and that I should be more careful.

Wow. We got lucky there.

Yeah, luck.

The shadows cast by the towering lights fell over her as she put down her pen. She smiled a bit and looked at the two approaching men. The man bent over to pick up the basketball and the sweat dripped off his stern shoulder. White light silhouetted his dark skin and left a chill in Kelly's arms. He raised his cold eyes and stared right at her. He was close enough that she could smell a mixture of Adidas cologne and body odor. It was a scent that would define her life.

Where'd your friends go?

He smiled at her and straightened his back. He tossed the ball from hand to hand. His trunks were worn low and she could see the tone line between his abdomen and pelvis. His underwear waistband was fully exposed. So much that she could read the brand name typed across it. She sat frozen with fear. They just left right?

Yeah, they'll be right back. Just to WaWa.

He covered her mouth and dropped the basketball in a millisecond. Her eyes bulged and she slid to the ground. She was as quiet as the wind though her mind wanted to scream. He took his other arm and wrapped it around her throat. He raised her to her feet.

Just be quiet, he said. She was having trouble breathing through her nose, which forced her to gag, and the tears had already begun to pour. He kept one hand over her mouth and groped her breast, then her stomach and finally between her legs.

No, not here. The Puerto Rican guy approached her and got right up in front of her. Come on let's go. He led the way toward the dark path. He followed with her in his arms. She struggled as much as she could but she weighed 110 pounds. The third guy picked up the basketball and followed a mid-leveled distance behind them.

One of her sandals fell off as she dug her feet into the dirt and tree stumps. She began to fight with all of her might and flailed her arms wildly. It was so dark that the men didn't even know where they were going. They went down a path that wasn't even there and broke into a clearing. It was a clearing about twenty feet wide littered with old rubber tires and empty beer cans. Light shined in from the court lights about thirty or forty yards away. There was a dirty twin sized mattress that lay against a tree horizontally.

Over here. The Puerto-Rican went to the mattress and pushed it to the ground. He forced her down to her knees and kept a tight grip on her from behind. He got close to her ear. If you scream I'm gonna punch your teeth in, you understand. She knelt sobbing and moaning. He let her mouth go and lowered his hands to her jean shorts and began to unbutton them. She dove on the mattress and spun to her back and screamed her lungs out, HELP! HELP ME! SOMEBODY HELP...

That wasn't a good idea. The Puerto-Rican grabbed her head and held it firm. The black man jabbed her straight in the face with his open palm.

Look what you did now, huh? She cried and let out a bellowing grunt. The pain shot through her heart as she knew this may be her last few moments of life. She tendered her mind and prayed for god to help her. He unzipped her jean shorts and pulled them completely off.

Yeah, now we're talking. Said the lookout voice from behind. He peered over his shoulder to see her half naked beaten body. Blood had begun to run off the side of her cheek from her nose.

Todd Bailey

THE COURTS

Todd Bailey

V

I have this recurring dream that the phone rings, I pick it up and it's a girl on the other end of the line. She tells me she misses me and wants to see me. It's been so long since we've talked she says. I hang up the phone and walk around in the bedroom I grew up in. Seconds later the phone rings again and I pick it up and ask, why are you calling me? She asks why I hung up on her and tells me she's got something to tell me.

THE COURTS

In the dream I know the feeling of who she is. She remains nameless throughout but I know that we were together at sometime. She tells me that she's pregnant and wants to get together to talk. I hang up the phone and pace about my bedroom some more. The phone rings a third time and it is a girlfriend of hers that I am also friends with and she tells me I need to speak with the girl who continues to call me. I tell her that I don't even know who she is and she tells me at this point that the girl has a two-year-old son who looks just like me and is mine.

I know that we were together at that point of my life but still run away and hang up the phone. I hang up the phone for the last time and climb out of my bedroom window and get into my sister's blue Pontiac Sunbird and drive for days. I end up in Tulsa, Oklahoma, on a park bench sitting next to a homeless man. He looks at me and speaks through his nappy grey beard. You should've talked to the girl on the phone, he says. Then I wake up feeling like I ran a marathon.

Sometimes the dream is different and it's not that I fathered an illegitimate child but that I killed a man. Again, I deny it and run. I may end up on a Greyhound bus but I always end up on that same bench in the same city with the same man.

A dream is defined as a series of mental images and emotions that happen during sleep. Everybody has them, and every once and a while people will tell you they had a dream last night. I guess if they are telling you the dream then it was strong enough for them to remember. Some dreams remain in your conscience, burned forever. Funny, how you can have a series of images and emotions that never really happened stick with you for life, but you can't remember your 25th birthday party or a random day or event in your life.

THE COURTS

The main living room at SIO had three couches and a dining room table with some chairs. The windows were covered with some sort of heavy board paper and painters tape. Thunder sat on the rug that had decades of stains. He stretched his hind legs and let out a huge yawn. Chaps sat in the only easy chair and bent forward to scratch and rub the dog.

The boys had unpacked their bags upstairs in one of the bedrooms and Pfifer came out to rest from the long trip. McKenzie sat on the edge of the bed with his cell phone in his lap. He text messaged with Angie telling him they were there and he was OK. She replied that she was down at Senior Week with Devon, Morgan, Kelly and a few other girls and would be back the following week.

He tucked his phone into his gym bag and walked down the hall to drop off the box that his mother made for his brother. They opened it. Dry noodles, some new clothes, Hygiene products, a card with some cash and other odds and ends. He put the cash in his top drawer and they headed down the stairs to the living room.

Lynn had shown up with some of her friends and they were in the kitchen making Jell-O shots of sorts.

Man, I wish you were coming home this summer, McKenzie told his older brother.

Coaches have got me running a wrestling camp. I'll show you guys the campus tomorrow, maybe play some tennis or something.

Sounds good. Pfifer sat at the end of the leather couch with a beer on the armrest. It was getting close to ten o'clock and the house had filled up a bit. Lots of drinking and smoking and fraternity antics went on. The boys soaked it all in and stayed up all night. They went outside on the porch and hung out with some freshmen girls. Pfifer made out with one girl and retired to the room he was spending the night in with her. McKenzie sat with Jenn who was going to be a sophomore the following year. She had long straight red hair and made continuous passes at him.

He repeatedly turned her down on the porch. They took a walk and there was a large rock that sat atop the hill. They sat on the edge at three in the morning, talking about what they thought was really important stuff at the time. They lay down on the stone together and looked up at the sky. She rested her arm around his waist and they kissed a few times.

He told her he had a girlfriend back home and that she was suffocating him and that it was really over and it was just a matter of time. Jenn got up and said she was cold and tired and that she was going back to the house. The mosquitoes were biting them. That made him worry about Kelly.

He got up with her and walked down the hill. Crickets shrieked in the woods. The grass was already wet. Inside the house Travis was spread out on the floor face down. Asleep. Someone else was lying on the couch watching Ren and Stimpy on the TV but he didn't know who it was. They crossed the room and climbed the stairs.

They got in the room, stripped down to their underwear and climbed under the sheets. No more words were said that night.

The boys got some breakfast in the morning and headed through the campus to the tennis courts by ten in the morning. Travis and Mick highlighted the walk with stories of the past year. The campus was full of winding pathways over acres of open land.

Brick dormitories and classroom buildings lined the walkway. There was still a good amount of foot traffic and students on bikes going by.

They passed a pond with a gazebo off the bank. A fountain recycled water over thirty feet high in the middle. A bulletin post with posters and clippings for *roommates wanted* caught McKenzie's eye. College was a few months away and it was to be a fresh start for him.

Coming over the hill they could see the tennis courts. There were two gated complexes with eight courts in each. They were empty. It was still early enough that it hadn't broken into the eighties.

Play doubles?

Yeah.

Travis and me verse you two. Said Pfifer. OK?

Sure. Travis didn't look to be much of an athlete. He wasn't much coordinated and he didn't dress the part. They opened the metal lock on the gate and entered the courts. McKenzie ran around the courts mimicking a championship Wimbledon run and was eager to hit some balls with his big brother. By the time they had finished warming up, Travis had already hit two balls over the gate. He went out to get them.

I could get used to this. McKenzie said.

Tell me about it. Pfifer shouted. This is beautiful. You're living the dream here Mick. Travis hit the balls back into the court from outside. It was college life, what it should be. It was four guys just hanging on campus. Talking. Playing tennis. Pfifer got on Travis' case because he couldn't hit one ball in play. The McKenzie brothers were like a machine.

The time went too quick for McKenzie and he wondered if his brother felt the same. Before he knew it, the sun had peaked atop the clear blue sky and the air was thick again. They packed up the balls and racquets and threw out their trash. On the way out they noticed some other courts had filled up.

Lynn met up with the boys in the parking lot at the Blues Festival with a few of her friends, including the red head. They tailgated off the back of the Excel with the hatchback up. They had two coolers. One for beer and water and the other for food. The BBQ grill was flaming and the lawn chairs were already spread out. The sounds of muffled blues echoed from the music center just down the road.

McKenzie dropped his head back over the canvas chair and rubbed his eyes under his dark sunglasses. Relaxed. He smiled. Like the sounds of being on the beach.

I think this is G. Love right? Pfifer said.

I don't know, is it? Lynn replied. Yeah I think you're right.

They had no plans of paying the $39.95 ticket price and dealing with the crowds and vendors. They were perfectly content in the lot. They could come and go as they pleased. The red head got up to head to the Port-O-Pottie and the other girls got up as well.

Wait for me. Pfifer got up to take the walk and Travis went as well. The McKenzie Brothers sat alone and silent for a good fifteen seconds or so. The bond of brothers.

You having a good time? Mick asked.

Yeah. This is awesome. Peaceful.

Yeah, it's nice.

The end of a great blues song. The band stretched it out as long as they can. The drums pounding as the lead guitar played every note in the scale until it was an octave higher then you thought it could get. The sound of the fifty thousand people erupting into applause and chants.

Wow, listen to that crowd.

Amazing.

Yeah.

There's something I want to tell you.

Mick peeled his head off the chair and asked, what is it?

You have to promise you will never mention this again or say anything.

Of course I won't, I'm your brother.

Mick anticipated the worst. The band dropped back into another great number. McKenzie took a moment. His stomach was sick with anxiety. He got up to walk it off.

Come on, it can't be that bad. Mick had always been supportive and protective of his little brother. Throughout the toughest of times.

A couple of weeks ago. It was late one night. I shot and killed someone. He looked into his brother's eyes. Not too long.

What are you talking about? What do you mean you killed someone.

Just that. I pulled out a gun and shot this black fellow three times. Twice in the back and once in the chest. It was late at night. Dark. We were at the courts. I left. Went to Angie's house. When I got back everybody was gone. There was nobody left. I was looking for Pfifer and Kelly. I heard screams coming from the path. It was so dark.

What were you doing with a gun?

I've had it for a few months now. Just for protection.

From what?

Just some people.

Who?

Things are different since you left. So different. Kids pick on me. Call me fag or wus. And that's just the surface of it. It hurts my feelings.

I can't believe I'm hearing this.

Anyways, it was really dark and I'm running through the path and I can hear this rustling through a line of shrubs and I've got my gun out by this point.

When I came through I saw Kelly on the ground and these three fucking guys on top of her. It was sick I tell you man. It made me so angry.

I screamed at them to get off of her. They didn't see me at first and just told me to get the fuck out. I said GET THE FUCK OFF OF HER and I pointed the gun at one of them. One of them was Spanish and he said to take it easy. Nobody wants to get hurt or killed here. And that's the irony of it. This fucking piece of shit has the balls to tell me nobody needs to get hurt here. The one asshole just kept raping her. He didn't stop. I shot the other one in the chest. He fell right to the ground and wheezed like he had the wind knocked out of him and rolled onto his stomach. I shot him two more times in the back. That got him off of her. He pulled his shorts back up and he ran off with the Spanish dude. Do you remember Kelly Sanchez?

Yeah. The black hair. In the Drama Club with you right?

Right. She laid there on her back. Naked. Sobbing and Bleeding. Her face was black and blue. And there was this fucking piece of shit dead. Laying a few feet from us. I asked her if she was all right and if I could help her and what we should do. She didn't want anybody to know about it. We sat in the woods for hours. Mostly in silence. We saw her friends come back with Pfifer looking for her and then they left. I called him on my cell and told him she came over Angie's and we would walk home from there.

She cried the whole night and I held her. When she couldn't cry anymore I got up. The sun started to rise and I pulled him deeper into the woods. I dragged a mattress that was there and covered him up.

Jesus Christ Brad, You're serious. Does anybody know about this? He pulled forward on his lawn chair and lifted his shades.

Me, Kelly, Pfifer and you.

Tim does know?

I told him the next day. We've been covering this up. The three of us. Just not telling anybody.

And the dead guy?

Pretty much washed over at this point. At least I hope. The cops found him and questioned his friends.

They denied that they new anything about it. Didn't even comment to the paper.

McKenzie stood there in the dead of heat with his heart poured out on his brother. Tears fell down his cheek and his brother held him. He sobbed deeply into his shoulder. He grabbed the back of his head and tugged at his hair. I don't know what to do, he confessed.

You'll be all right. Were not going to do a thing. OK, you hear me? You don't tell one person about this for the rest of your life. He pulled his head back and stared directly into his soaked eyes. Not one person. Not even Mom & Dad.

He carried his body differently the rest of the day. He smiled in conversation but no real laughter came out of it. His voice was scratchy and echoed inside. He felt vertigo at times. And had to sit down for a moment. He took an extra Xanax and told himself to chill out. He would pace around the car smoking cigarettes. In what seemed like an eternity he had convinced himself he couldn't breathe or swallow and was going to die. He thought he might pass out from the anxiety until the medication kicked in.

The crew collected their belongings, folded up the chairs and packed the grill in the back of the Excel. They tied down the hatchback so the grill rested half out of the back. Travis sat in the back with one hand on it for security. They beat the traffic out and promised to meet up at the house that night.

By the time they came up on the driveway it was dark. Pfifer and Travis were asleep in the back.

McKenzie sat silent looking out at the countryside. The rear bumber or suspension system bottomed out coming up the road and the car yakked out of pain. The McKenzie brothers let out a nervous laugh as he turned into the parking space next to the Jeep under a large Dogwood.

At night they sat out back over acres of open plains and shot off the fireworks. The bottle rockets screamed through the night sky and popped at the end. Roman candles sparkled and shells topped off with patterns of purple and red. They lit a campfire and laid out under the clear sky. Thunder chased sticks that were tossed across the field and ran the night through. The crisp spring night air cleared away the pollen and the crickets scraped off in the distance.

Chaps sat on an old NFL blanket and thumbed through a version of Bob Dylan's *Like a Rolling Stone*. His voice was broken between the melody lines and harmony. He wasn't the best of singers but it was in key. Lynn sat between Mick's legs and rested on his chest with a college sweatshirt on. The sleeves were too long and cuffed up over her fingers. Mick brushed through her hair and looked on at Chaps.

McKenzie scrolled through his phone texting Angie. She told him she was having a good time down the shore and that she missed him. When you get back we can talk about what we are going to do.

There's nothing to talk about. It is what it is.

You just want to throw away two years?

It's not throwing it away. You'll be at school and so will I. We'll try and keep in touch. See what happens.

That sounds like Pfifer talking.

Whatever.

Yeah, whatever.

It was one of those nights. The subtle nuances of exploration were eminent. He was completely relaxed. They sat in a circle next to the bon-fire. Chaps put his guitar in the brown case and gathered everyone's attention. The group talked for an hour or so. Everybody was at one with each other. They settled in to play a game that he called *The Magic Circle*.

More of just a personal confession where one person would ask a question and everyone in the circle would take turns answering the question. The only rules were to be honest and to trust one another. Nothing was to leave the circle. And no stone was to be left unturned. Questions ranged from; where was the weirdest place you had sex, to if you could live in any space in time, when would you live?

The red head took the cake on the sex question confessing she had once screwed a guy in the nurses' bathroom at her high school back home. Travis said he would have loved to have lived in the Wild Wild West. Time stood still as eight people dug into their own emotions and memories and brought them to words. Natural therapy.

Pfifer and the freshman were putting on their own public display of affection. She rested her head on his shoulder and nibbled lightly. Eventually they broke off down the hill. The coldness dug into McKenzie's skin and he stood up and called it a night. The red head followed him off and into the house loosely.

What are you going to do? Said Lynn. Now that you've graduated.

Chaps smiled at the uncertainty of life and challenged himself to impress. I think I'm going to stay in town for a while. I've got the web site and my friends and I'm living comfortably. See, I've got this degree in business and that part of my life is over. I've finished it.

Mick sat looking on with candor. His fingers picked and peeled at a beer label wrapper till it shred to pieces. Chaps had mentored him and was a main reason why he had come to that school. He was recruited hard and he took a grand liking toward him. Sure, the athletics were one of the nations best and the full ride was the perk he needed but Chaps treated him just like anybody else. Like a friend. A good one at that.

The tide pushed far away from the beach. The sand scalded their feet as they walked over the dunes and down toward the ocean. Each girl carried a beach bag. They kicked sand up. The seagulls were just overhead and shrieked loudly. They stayed off the main tourist drag and lay out on *Surfers Beach*. Devon, Morgan and Angie were the first to arrive. They plotted out the spot, spread out long beach towels and took off their cover-ups. They laid under the sun baking and sipping water. They ate fruit salad from a Tupperware container.

Off the beach were parking spaces full of cars. It was difficult to find an open space. As they drove by, one of the girls noticed Morgan's Cabriolet. They pulled in to a space a block off the beach and walked up. Kelly noticed the girls just down the beach. They walked through a maze of make shift beach sites. Umbrellas and sand castles. The girls plopped down all of their gear.

Hey. Morgan said.

Hi, how's it going? Kelly replied. This is gorgeous.

Yeah, it's nice.

She motioned at the school of surfers riding the breakers. Lot's of eye candy out here too. Kelly laughed a bit then spread out and sat Indian Style. A young family of four was a few feet away from them. Angie sat staring at the boy and girl playing. Their parents were probably late twenties or early thirties. An attractive couple. The All-American family. The little girl was around three years old and she ran about the beach in her little butterfly bikini. She played with some boys that were racing to the ocean with buckets, filling up with salt water and rushing back. The little girl would take her bucket over to the boys and have them fill it up for her. She smiled and laughed then brought each full back to a blow up baby pool that her brother was in. He was under a year old with straight blonde hair. The cutest kids in the world.

She watched their every move as she text messaged on her phone. The mother and father had their hands full. The father played in the sand making a three story sand castle with a moat and the mother took pictures and shot video. She rolled onto her back and shut her eyes. Kelly looked her over, what's wrong?

Oh, I don't know. Brad I guess.

I thought it was over. You guys ended it right?

Yeah, before he left we got together at my graduation party. I know it was a mistake and now he's... I don't know. Whatever.

Oh god just let it go. Kelly said with temperament. If you love him set him free and if it is meant to be then he will come back. Besides, you're going to be eighteen years old. It's not like you're getting married or anything. Enjoy life.

Whatever Kelly. She turned on her side and curled up a bit. Kelly put sun tan lotion on and laid on her stomach. Several surfers came up to the girls and flirted with them. They laughed and flirted back. Morgan was always interested in making idle chitchat with random guys. She batted her lashes and giggled at high pitches. Devon pulled her back to reality when they asked them to come to their house later that night for a party.

Thanks but no thanks, this is a girls only Senior Week. No Boys!

I don't know Devon; maybe we can make an exception. The guys continued with their hunt until she pacified them with a maybe. She had no intention of meeting up. Angie kept her eyes closed and smiled at the possibility. The father of the family peered over at the teens and spoke to his wife.

Remember being that young? Not a care in the world?

Yeah. She wrestled a bottle into the baby's mouth as he climbed over her.

On the contrary, Angie looked on in awe of the family. She sat up and looked over her skin for signs of any shading and to sip water from a bottle. What's the bruise from Kelly? She poked her finger into the back of her thigh. Kelly startled and got up to her knees. She was quite off guard and her anxiety rushed like a mighty river. She twisted her leg in an angle to observe. She hadn't noticed it before. The backs of her thighs were still badly bruised. The center almost black and the surrounding area was a yellowish brown. It was a large bruise almost four inches wide.

Don't poke at me! She was defensive. The anger filled her eyes and Angie was terrified.

Relax, I'm sorry, god.

What happened? Devon and the girls turned their attention to her.

I just touched the bruise on her thigh as a joke and asked what the bruise was from.

That hurt. Do not touch me. She stood up, put on her shorts that covered the mark and walked over the dunes. By the time she reached the parking lot she was in tears. She had hoped she hadn't caused too much of a scene where somebody would have followed her.

That night there was a heavy rain that came up from the Carolina's. Lightning filled the sky with bright blue flashes. She kept to herself for the rest of the week. Her restless sleep could not shake the nightmares. She woke each morning with emptiness. The following Wednesday she cut her trip early, said her goodbyes and drove home. She sat silent in her car without the radio. The passing Pinelands of route 206 streaked with a windswept Gaussian blur.

Pfifer and McKenzie had been home for three days retreating in the end of spring. It had rained on and off for the past five. When McKenzie got the call from her to come out he turned off the TV and went to the back shed behind his parents house.

He sifted through the clutter in the dark and pulled out his mountain bike. He peddled through the sections drives and inlets.

On the main road toward Five Points was the Golden Dawn Diner. The lights changed to let oncoming traffic yield to the left and he crossed the busy intersection. He cashed a check at the Check Cashing office and paid the six percent fee. He was left with just over two hundred dollars that he folded into his wallet. He had earned the money working at a local garage door warehouse. Wrapping and prepping garage doors for contractors. The metal tracks left cuts in his shins and fingers.

When he came out of the building it had begun to rain again. He raced across the lot to the diner. The bike rack had just one other bike locked to it. An ancient ten-speed with curved handlebars. He parked his bike in the rack and walked up the ramp. Inside was an older Greek women who asked if he needed a table. He mentioned he was meeting someone here and spotted her at a window booth. She was hunched over the table. Her stark black hair covered a portion of her face including her eyes.

He sat across from her. Hello.

Hey.

How are you?

I'm OK.

Yeah? I've been worried about you.

Did you want to see a menu? She handed him a menu that was over two feet high. The cover had stains on the plastic and was sticky. He picked out a pork roll and cheese on a Kaiser and a diet coke. Kelly had a club sandwich. The food was diner food.

How was the shore?

It was nice. Angie is a bitch. She gets under my skin. Like, who does she think she is?

He pulled his cigarette pack out and placed it on the table for the box to dry. The cigarette he lit had a few damp spots on it but it dragged just fine. She's a trip isn't she?

I don't know how you put up with her.

Tell me about it.

She still loves you, you know.

You think?

I know. That's all she talked about the whole week. Brad said this. Brad did that. You made the right decision. She hooked up with some random guy one night. She was drinking and acting like she was holding court or something. This little twig was all about her. Put her on a pedestal or something. I mean, she's pretty but her personality is for shit.

Their food came and they ate. Conversation came easy with her. Her club sandwich sat on her plate with just a few bites in it. She picked at the French Fries and ate the coleslaw.

I figured she would hook up with someone. She's very self-loathing.

Have you heard anything? Kelly probed him. She wanted more than anything for him to understand that she appreciated him.

No. Absolutely nothing. Not a word about it from anyone. I want you to know, that whatever you decide, about all of this, I'm completely behind you. One hundred percent.

I know. My mind is made up though. I want to move on. However that comes. I don't know. But, I don't want to go to the cops and I'm OK with that. Brad, what you did was more then any retribution I could ask for. For those other assholes to be living with the fear is all I need. For the rest of their lives they have to look at themselves in the mirror. One day they may have kids. Even a little girl and they'll have to face their daughter's eyes each and every day knowing what kind of scum they truly are.

McKenzie finished off his sandwich and sat back in the vinyl booth. He kicked one of his sneakers off and crossed his legs under the table. I just wish none of this ever happened.

I know.

Kelly, I love you. You are one of my best friends, you're the most decent person that I know and I am so sorry.

I know. I am too. She pulled her hair back over her ear and tucked her chin down. She stared at her plate.

I want to kill the other two.

You can't.

I could find them. Hunt them down and take them out too.

No, you can't. I don't want you to do that.

I know you don't want me to, but I think I want to.

I'd hate you forever.

THE COURTS

VI

I've heard about lucky people. Maybe on a 60 Minutes special or a Dateline show. There truly are Lucky and Unlucky people and it may begin with positive thinking. Lucky People know where they will end up but they just may not know how they will get there. They generally always get there though. If you feel that you are a lucky person then good things will come. Like self-help but a little more unscientific.

They showed these studies where they put self-proclaimed lucky and unlucky people in a coffee shop. The experiment was to see who new patrons were drawn to. Most of the time they sat near or next to the self proclaimed lucky person. You never know about the source and with film editing this day and age you can make viewers perceive what ever you want them to. Check out Michael Moore's mockumentary Fahrenheit 911 in which the source was completely altered and manipulated in the film for his own personal views.

I'm no right wing extremist but I am a general believer in fundamentalism. I also think that putting someone on camera without that person knowing what the end product is trying to achieve can bring on disastrous results. The State of the Union is tense with the Mid-East war, immigration and the current state of healthcare. I'm even concerned about Social Security. Choosing a new president will not solve any of these issues.

The presidential position is more of a symbol of strength. All the Bush bashing has more of a negative international effect then the man himself.

We're lucky to have a democracy where we can freely elect our public servants. We're lucky to have the independence to openly discuss our views and champion policies of change. We're lucky to have support systems in place that combat against poverty, alcoholism, disease and domestic issues.

I'm lucky to be on this continent. In this country. I'll spend my entire life living on the mainland, probably the mid-Atlantic. I'll always experience true season changes. At least until the polar caps completely melt over.

I read about making your own luck in an unlucky world that lucky people are more open minded to change that is around them. They don't get stuck in routines and they often pursue alternate methods of going about their own day.

There was a researcher who had subjects thumb through a newspaper and he told them to count the amount of photographs in the paper. It was a menial task. Count the photos and tell me how many photos at the end.

They'd thumb through the paper counting and on the third page there was an advertisement right next to a photo that read "STOP COUNTING - THERE ARE 43 PHOTOS IN THIS NEWSPAPER. - TELL THE EXPERIMENTER YOU'VE SEEN THIS AND WIN 150 POUNDS".

The lucky people would stop and ask for the money. The unlucky would continue through to the end. Whether it was tricking the mind or gauging ones openness to opportunity is up for debate, but it is certainly an interesting experiment. I've won the lottery before. The Daily Number boxed. Came out to $89. I've had other instances of luck and consider myself lucky. When I found out I was having a baby girl I knew I was lucky. And when I found out I was having a baby boy I knew I was truly blessed.

One night I was driving over a friend of mine's house in my black 2000 Blazer. I traveled in the left lane and was approaching a stop light before entering I-95 in Bristol, PA. I was on my cell with my wife when out of my right field of vision I saw this old white Jeep Cherokee making an illegal U turn from two lanes over. He clipped a sedan to my right and then I T-Boned into the driver door. My cell phone fell to the floor as I came to rest on the median.

I looked up to see three black juveniles scrambling to get out of the passenger side and run. Before I could even think I picked up my phone and told my wife I was just in an accident. There were already several police cars and a helicopter. The kids had stolen the car and were involved in a police chase. I described the scene to my wife, saying it was like Beirut. There was a moment that I thought about getting out and chasing them down with a golf club from my back seat but I considered myself lucky to not have been hurt.

I followed up the accident with physical therapy and it turns out, one of the kids that were arrested was the son of a classmate of mine from high school. About thirteen thousand dollars later and active lower lumbar strain I am surviving.

Most recently I took PNC Bank to smalls claims court to dispute an $89 claim for insufficient fees and early termination. I showed up at the courthouse and had to plead a proof case in front of a judge. The judge said, "You're suing PNC Bank for $89? I gotta hear this". By the end of my litigation I had the judge, clerks and the entire courtroom rallying behind my initiative to stick one to the man. I always wanted to sue somebody and now I had succeeded against a company worth over 2 trillion in total fund assets.

I'm lucky to have been able to travel in my life. Over 23 states in the country as well as many Caribbean islands and Canada. We're lucky to have world-class cities and tourist destinations within our reach. The wealth of this country will always be its inhabitants. The test of our society is to maintain its integrity.

The dining room was a converted garage with vaulted ceilings and a bubbled skylight. There was caulk around the window to prevent future leaks. The ceiling was covered with wood and stained in a rich cherry brown. The space had custom fabricated vertical windows, which let in the western sunset. Artwork lined the adjacent walls consisting of owls, wicker and outdoor scenes.

There was a half wall that connected to the kitchen and McKenzie could see his mother preparing dinner at the stove. His father sat at the head of the table with the newspaper in front of him.

The emptiness poured out from the silence. He turned the pages of the paper and they rustled like a freight train. The pots on the stove banged. She rested a serving dish on the bright orange countertops that were still left from the seventies. He took his time to stare at each piece of the room. He gnawed at a dinner roll and sipped iced water from a tinted tumbler. There would be no fights tonight. He was a man at the end of his sentence. A few days and he would be released into the free world.

The taste of college that he had with his brother was all he needed to get through the summer. He minded his manners as best he could. Stayed out of trouble and finished up summer school. He spent most of his time with Pfifer playing volleyball or wiffleball at his new apartment. Pfifer would stay back and go to the local community college for two years.

He walked the main drag of New Hope with Kelly a couple times. They had their own spot down behind the local Playhouse. There was a nice shaded area where they could see the bridge that crossed the river to Lambertville. It was quiet. The town itself hustled with art and culture and she fit right in. She loved its hometown shops and restaurants. They talked several times about what had happened and what they expected from college in the upcoming year. Their friendship blossomed.

When the time came, he took the ride straight across the state with his parents. They checked into a hotel for the night. One last night and then free roam on the town. It was a dark room and he could hear every breath his mother and father took. It was a long night in the dark.

In the morning they crossed the river and came into downtown Pittsburgh. It was a bustling city. Women walked in power suits and sneakers. They toured the Point and the Incline and had breakfast. The conservatory sat in the heart of the city and his dormitory was twenty stories high. He registered for his classes and got his photo ID and meal plan.

He had to take some regular classes so he took English, Art History and Earth Science. Other then that it was all Acting. He got his schedule, which would take him out to the Oakland section by University of Pitt. That's where the Playhouse was.

Later that night he checked in on Kelly's dorm. She was on an all girls floor, number 12. He was on a coed, number 16. He knocked on the door. She answered in a T-Shirt and sweats. Hey.

How you doing?

We made it huh?

Yeah, here we are.

Come on in. He came into the room to see crazy drawings she had done hung up everywhere. Lot's of dark colors. Two single beds. The other side of the room had not been claimed yet.

Pretty cool. Looks like you are all settled in.

Yeah, pretty much. No roommate yet. I'm kind of nervous about that.

I hear you. I met mine. He's alright. Kind of a jock. He's not in theatre. That's all right though. He's from Pittsburgh. You want to take a walk?

Yeah, sure. Just let me pull up my hair real quick. She went into the bathroom and he looked out her window. He could see over the Point, where the three rivers met.

They explored the first few floors and found a café and the bookstore. On the second floor were several dance studios that were filled to capacity. Men and women sweating from dancing. They watched a while and had never seen anything like it before. They were extremely good at what they did.

Down the hall was the mailroom with a full line of mailboxes. He checked in and got his mail key. They ventured out onto the street and headed down to the point. On the way they passed a few fast food chains and some delis. At the point they crossed a historical fort and ventured through a park. At the edge they rested against a rail and looked out on the mighty rivers. It was a clean city. It was a clean slate.

The first few weeks of college flew by. Classes were interesting. He went to mostly all of them. He especially loved the Acting class where he could show his talent off. He studied the method and absorbed the sensory exercises with ease.

He made friends easily. Not so easy for Kelly, but she always had him. They stuck together closely. Nights and weekends, they went to parties and shows around town with Kelly's roommate Olivia.

Like anything before, McKenzie lost interest and began to slip from his enthusiasm. He cursed out a teacher in a Stage Movement class and got tossed out of class. He sat around goofing off and not working and got tossed out of his Stage Management class. He went to Earth Science three times for the whole semester and failed the final with ease. He was on probation of losing his scholarship within three months.

The second semester would be a second chance. He'd get a new roommate, another acting student, Eric Simpson. The two of them had been spending much of the first semester getting to know each other. They shared a great interest in experimenting with drugs, acting in indie films and taking each day as it came. Eric kept up with his studies while McKenzie slept in each day.

Kelly's roommate was a girl named Olivia from just outside of Lancaster, PA. She was a sweet and innocent girl who had never even been out of her hometown before. McKenzie took a liking to her right away. They would spend hours down at the café talking about where they had come from and what they wanted to do.

When he came to visit her in their dorm room it was the funniest thing. There was a stark contrast between Kelly's darkness and Olivia's photos of flowers and ballerinas.

One night, just before Christmas break, McKenzie and Olivia crossed the Smithfield Street Bridge with Kelly and Simpson. The oldest bridge in Alleghany County was narrow and the ice sheet was beginning to melt. Must have been just over forty degrees. Across the river they stopped at Station Square and had dinner. They climbed the side of the mountain to the white house, which was an off campus residence.

They came into the home and it was dark. There were a good amount of students that he didn't know. A Janis Joplin album ran on a loop at peak volume. He couldn't even hear Olivia when she said she loved this song.

They crossed an empty room lit up by candles. There were three or four kids sitting against the wall. They watched them as they walked by. In the hallway by the stairs there was a girl in her bra and panties and another guy in just his shorts. They were making out against the mirror by the side door.

Up the stairs a hall light was on and they could smell the sweet scent of marijuana. Simpson opened the bedroom door and walked in. The other three followed and crowded by the open bedroom door.

There was what looked like a hippie guy sitting on the floor with a hookah in front of him. He sat smoking. Two girls on the bed seemed dazed as they carried an empty smile. At the desk, Tyler rose and smiled.

Hey. He was an exact twin of Adam Sandler except always stoned. He was likeable. How you doing Eric?

Good. Just came by to see what was up, ya know?

You got it. Did you need some pot?

Yeah, we'd like an ounce if you got it.

Yeah, I got it. He sat down at his desk and began to weigh it out for him. How about some acid? I got this good stuff. Only $5 a hit. He pulled a sheet of tin foil out which had a strip of paper and showed it to them.

No, I don't think so. But thanks. McKenzie looked at the acid and wondered of its effects. He hadn't tried anything like that before and had only heard about it from friends. Pfifer told him that he took it once and was so bugged out that he almost jumped out of a window and that he thought his heart was going to stop.

He looked at the girls on the bed and knew them both. They lived on his floor and were always partying. He didn't know their majors or where they were from but had a pretty good idea of their names. He said hello.

What are you guys doing tonight? One of them asked.

We're going down to the South Side to walk around a bit. See what's going on.

Did you want a hit of this? The hippie on the ground asked?

Sure, Simpson took the hookah from him and after a brief tutorial he smoked it. It produced an exuberant amount of smoke that poured out of his mouth and nose. It was a cloud that consumed him. The girls didn't smoke any and were even getting a bit uncomfortable of the whole scene.

Simpson paid him $100 for the ounce and they left the house. By the time they broke out onto the street Simpson's heart was racing and he was high.

What was that? Olivia said.

I think they were all tripping. Kelly laughed. It's like they were zombies or something. What complete wastoids.

Did you see those two people were just about naked in the middle of the hall? Did you see that?

Yeah. They were definitely on something. Tyler's nice.

Yeah he is, Olivia said. He loves the weed though, huh?

He sure does. Kelly called for a taxi on her cell phone. They got to Carson St. and paid the driver. The Lava Lounge was a hip little place to grab a booth, drink and listen to music. They spent two hours chatting. The place was full of a college crowd and 80's music.

I had a girlfriend back home. Pretty much throughout high school. We met the first day of school and were together all three years.

What happened? Olivia asked.

She was going to a state college and I was coming here with Kelly. We grew apart. It's kind of sad. In our senior year we knew it was happening and we started fighting all the time. It's too hard, ya know? You're only eighteen years old and you're expecting to make a long-term commitment.

I can certainly understand that. I was in the same boat. My boyfriend was a little obsessed though. He couldn't handle the distance. He got violent even. One night my dad had to throw him out of our house because he was screaming, "you're going to go to college and forget all about me. You're gonna fall in love and fuck some guy". It was horrible. I cried the whole night.

My god.

My dad had to come down in to the basement and he asked him to leave and he called my dad an asshole and you don't call my dad an asshole. I mean, he had gone out of his way for this kid in the past. He got him out of trouble, gave him a job at my dad's quarry. And this is how he repaid him?

Sounds like a real winner.

Yeah, tell me about it. So, high school could not end soon enough. And now here we are.

Yeah, and you're homesick like a dog.

I know. I miss my friends, my grandma and my parents.

You're doing great though. It's almost Christmas. You'll be home in a few days for break. I'll miss you though.

I know. You're sweet.

And you can come visit over Christmas, meet the family. That'd be nice.

I think I'm going to do that. That'll be cool.

The lights came up in the place and they got up to leave. Kelly and Simpson had spent most of the night at the bar. He couldn't have been more of a gentleman. He had social skills and was always polite. They came out of the bar and decided to walk the two or three miles and save the money. They all had a good beer buzz going and were having too good a night to let a little wind chill take it away.

They got to the blue bridge by quarter after two and started to cross. Trucks whizzed by and the steel shook with them. It was a good ten degrees colder over the water. Across the street there was some scaffolding. Part of a restoration effort.

I'm going up. Simpson jumped the railing, crossed the street and began to scale the cold pipe.

He's nuts. Kelly looked on and was intrigued. It's a crazy thing when you get that rush to be fearless. Get down from there.

I'm going. McKenzie climbed over the fence. His sneaker laces got caught on the top of the rail and he crashed to the cement road and cracked down on his elbow. The alcohol in his system and the parka he had on was enough padding to break his fall. He streaked across the street and was a body length behind him.

The wind rustled through the metal and they swayed a few feet each way. They sat atop the scaffolding at 2:30 in the morning, a good 200 feet above the Monongahela River. Cold breath poured out of their mouths. Simpson laid on his back in pure exhilaration.

Goddamn. McKenzie stood with pride. He raised his arms above his head. Isn't it beautiful? He screamed in a primal fashion.

They're freakin' crazy. Kelly said.

I know. Get down from there.

This is the life McKenzie. Nobody can touch us here. We could just stay up here forever.

There was no parade when he got home that night but the buzz had grown so much in the town that several reporters greeted him at the airport when he landed. Mostly local newspapers and the college TV station. Mick's coaches walked by his side as they came up the ramp and were all but dead tired.

They clapped for him as he came up and he smiled out of exhaustion. It was a good feeling to have strangers recognize you for your accomplishment. He had continued his quest for a national championship falling short at the Midlands. He was the college's first All-American wrestler and had 37 wins that year.

Welcome home Mick, said one reporter.

Thanks.

Seventh place isn't too bad at all. Congratulations. Are you happy with the season you had?

Yes, I'm very happy. I think we gave it a good run and I hope to be in the finals next year.

Your first true season on the mat at the college level, how would you sum it up?

Well, it's very competitive. The wrestlers are big and strong and well trained. I've gotta work harder over the next year and come up bigger. I know I will. My coaches are behind me and so is the school so I know we'll give it an even better run next season.

They ran some more questions by him and put his words on cassette. The next day there was a big picture of him on the front page of the school paper, the local paper and even the Philadelphia Inquirer. Front page. For a sophomore to run up such a good year was quite special.

He woke up in the room at the frat house with Travis at the foot of his bed. His back was to him and he was hunched over the desk. He heard him snorting a line of something or other. Travis kicked his head back and clucked his throat from the immediate drip.

Hey.

Yo, welcome home Mick. Tough loss but I think you did awesome man. You're on the front page of the paper.

Oh yeah? Thanks.

You'll get'em next year, right?

Yeah. Hopefully. He got out of bed and jumped in the shower. His body was bruised and sore. His bones pierced through his skin as much as his oversized muscles did. The bandage on his ear had flopped off on one side in his sleep.

Tonight we're going out to The Smithson. Little celebration for you. What do you think about that?

OK. Mick took a good long hot shower. He came out of the bathroom and Travis was gone.

That winter was especially cold. When Mick got home the family was all there. Mr. McKenzie had the Christmas lights already strung up and his mom had her Lennox snowmen placed all over the house. The tin bucket was full of ice and had five bottles of wine chilling.

His sister Cheryl and her fiancé Anthony were there. He had two children from a previous marriage and they were the life of the party. Children somehow drew all of the tension away from family affairs. Anthony was an Italian restaurant owner and was eager to meet the entire family.

His cousins, uncles, aunts and some family friends were there. Some huddled around the TV and talked football and others mingled about the place. There was no lack of conversation. Coming into the McKenzie's house was like entering a royal palace. Whoever saw you first would shout your name and greet you with as big a smile as they could muster. Within five minutes a glass of wine or a cold beer was in your hand.

The aroma of Mr. McKenzie's award winning meatballs had been slow cooking for a couple of hours now and it filled the home with a holiday smell. They exchanged some gifts with each other.

How's school going? Mick asked.

It's going good. Acting classes are good. They don't let me audition for any shows until next year so it's a bit boring.

Like red shirting?

Yeah, exactly. Mick, this is my girlfriend Olivia.

Hi.

Hello. Nice to meet you.

She goes to school with me.

Oh yeah? Are you in theatre too?

No, I'm a dance major.

That's pretty cool.

Listen, we're going to meet up with Pfifer tonight if you want to come out.

Absolutely. Let's get through all of this first, though.

Christmas at the McKenzie's was always special. After dinner they played some party games. Anthony's teenage kids loved the time spent around the dinner table.

So, how did he ask you to marry him? McKenzie asked his sister.

Well. It was a Saturday. We were planning on going down to New Hope for the day. We stopped in for lunch at a bakery by his sister's house in Westampton. It was a nice day outside. We came back out to the truck and his truck wouldn't start which I thought was odd because he takes good care of it. Always changes the oil. He's got like OCD about that kind of stuff. Anyway. The truck wouldn't start and we had to call a taxi to get us back home. But when the taxi came it wasn't a cab. It was a limo. When the limo came he got down on his knee and asked me to marry him.

Ahh. That's sweet. Olivia said.

Yes, it was very nice. I said yes and we actually took the limo down to Atlantic City for the night. His sister came and picked up his truck.

Were you surprised?

Actually, yes. Very surprised. I had no clue and it was really romantic. The whole weekend was very special.

Were you nervous? She asked Anthony.

I was shaking. My palms were sweating. Oh god. Yes. I was very nervous.

Did he ask you for permission dad? Mick asked. Everybody let out a big laugh

Oh yeah he did. I said certainly. You're a good man and I wouldn't have it any other way. Take care of my daughter.

And I will. That might have been even more nerve wrecking but it was the right thing to do.

By the time his sister left and all of the relatives cleared out it was past nine o'clock. Olivia went into his old bedroom and got ready to go out for the night. He helped his mom clean up the dishes.

Wow. To what to owe for this? McKenzie smiled in pride. My baby is growing up.

Yeah. If independence has taught me anything it's that the laundry and dishes don't clean themselves. I actually enjoy cleaning now. It calms me. I love you mom.

Ahh. Thank you babe. I love you too.

I don't know that I've told you that in a while but thank you, for everything.

You're welcome. Well, we've had some tough times but that's part of growing up. That's the way life goes and we move on. It's what makes us stronger, ya know?

Yeah, I do.

Olivia drove that night, her car handled a little better than the Excel over the black ice. They pulled up Ivy Hill and stopped on the street outside of Pfifer's house. McKenzie tapped the horn four times in a rhythm that made it secret to the lifelong friends only. They saw his head peak out from the kitchen and he appeared from the front door a few moments later.

He came to the window. Yo, my pop has got some meatballs on; did you want to come in? McKenzie gestured and Olivia turned the car off. They went inside and introduced Olivia to his family. McKenzie was eager to get some more meatballs in him.

These are the second best meatballs in the world.

Oh yeah? Pfifer's dad made just as good a meatball as Mr. McKenzie did but family honor kept his rating to second best. He had two sandwiches while Mick talked about the wrestling season. Pfifer's mom showed Mick the picture of him from the Inquirer.

It was a picture of him from two years ago with several gold medals draped around his neck from a tournament in Japan that he wrestled in. He had this big grin on his face. The title read *McKenzie Makes a Sophomore Impression* and went on to talk about his entire season.

Sounds like you're doing pretty well up there. Pfifer's dad spoke with a high-pitched raspy voice. He had some damage to his throat from Vietnam. He was on disability as long as the McKenzie Brothers could remember.

They drove up the hill and out the back of the section, which led them to the main road. By the time they got to Bailey's Irish Pub the place was filled to the brim. Still they found a table with a crew that they went to high school with. Pitcher's of Lager were flowing. Olivia and McKenzie played darts across the bar. She flung her body at him and all but laid on him. They flirted throughout the night.

She looked brilliant under the neon glow of alcoholic signage. Her thick natural brown hair was curvy and full. He admired her complexion by rubbing his fingers over her high cheeks. While they waited for their next turn at the board she rested against him. He was leaned up against the wall. His arms wrapped around her waist.

Through the crowd of people he saw a slumped over man at a small two seater table. In front of him were a half drunk pitcher and an ashtray, filled to the brim with menthol cigarette buts. He noticed him earlier in the night but paid no mind. By now the occasional glares he caught from him were soaking into his subconscious.

It was a familiar sense and the fear chilled his very being. It was the other black guy from that night six months ago. The man got up abruptly and the foot of his chair shrieked on the tile. He stood tall, over six feet. He looked down at his table for quite a long time sensing eyes upon him. Then he carried himself across the bar and into the bathroom.

McKenzie stood there without a breath in his throat. The whole place turned silent upon him and he trembled at the thought of what might happen next.

Let's go back to the table. He told Olivia.

What? Are you sure?

Now. Let's go.

OK. What's wrong? He pulled her along by the hand and they raced toward Mick who sat at the table with Pfifer. He dropped in his seat.

Mick, one of the guys. From that night. He's here. His head beaded with sweat and his eyes were as open as could be.

What?

He's here. I just saw him. I think he saw me. I think he knows me and he's here.

Where?

He just went into the bathroom.

What's going on? Olivia began to get nervous as she leaned in to here their whispering.

I don't know what to do.

We gotta leave. Mick rose to his feet and pulled out a wad of cash. He dropped it on the table. Let's go.

What is going on? Olivia sat there at the table for a moment before McKenzie pleaded with her.

We've gotta get out of here. Trust me. We need to go now. She got up and they rushed toward the front door. He all but pushed her in front of him. The sound of the place picked up like white noise and forced his heart to race.

Outside of the bar it was cold with wind and light snow. Olivia's car couldn't have been any further away that night. McKenzie kept looking back at the door. Nothing. They got in the car and Olivia struggled a bit to get the key out.

Take your time. We're ok. A thud came upon the windshield followed by a face that was angry as hell. He pressed his palms on the glass and he could see the blood rush from his knuckles.

I'm gonna kill you. He screamed. Olivia let out a scream. McKenzie recognized him as the Puerto-Rican from that night.

Jesus Christ. Pfifer shouted. Lock your doors. Everybody lock their doors.

We should be killing this motherfucker. McKenzie shouted.

No. Just stay in the car. Pfifer said.

Oh my god, oh my god, oh my god.

I know who you are Brad McKenzie. It was a muffled scream that distorted in the present time. Like slowing down a record. McKenzie sat there staring at him. That moment will stay with him forever. Like the birth of a tumor in his brain, it would never go away.

Olivia turned the ignition and jerked the car into drive. The guy fell off the side of the car with one last punch to the door. His finger streaks left on the windshield. He came to a rest in an embankment. She turned around a row of cars toward the exit.

Oh shit. He's got a gun! McKenzie shouted. Go, go, go. Keep going.

In the rear, the dark shadow drew his hands down into his pants and raised a .38 caliber Smith and Wesson. As she spun out of the lot they heard a gunshot come from behind them. They gasped and screamed. Then another shot. She climbed up past 45 miles an hour within seconds and they escaped physically unscathed.

The car idled just behind an old tan Bronco. McKenzie got out and shut the door. He walked up the pathway and tucked his hands in the pocket of his jacket. The porch light was on by the time he got to the steps. Inside the window he could see Kelly.

Hey. What's going on?

Something bad. Why don't I tell you what happened. Can I come in?

Sure. She opened the screen door and he went inside. Her house was empty that night except for the cats. They scurried around the corner to see who was there. He sat in her living room and told her what happened and her eyes swelled up. He said it'd be best if she came out and told everybody in the car so that they had a better understanding of the circumstances and she agreed.

Pfifer and my brother already know. I'm sorry.

I figured. That's OK. I understand that. What are we going to do?

She got her jacket and locked the door behind her. They walked down to the car side-by-side and squeezed into the back seat.

Let's go. McKenzie said. Olivia looked in her mirror to see Kelly crying and feared the worst. Nothing could prepare her for what was next.

Todd Bailey

THE COURTS

VII

Justice was once wrapped up in a neat little bow tied on the door of a courthouse. Anytime I saw someone get questioned in a courtroom I automatically judged them as guilty. Clarence Thomas. Oliver North. Rodney King. Growing up in post Generation X, those are the main ones. But then I wonder if the media spoonfed them to me as stories to rally behind.

Did you ever know someone that was so stubborn on their own views and morals that they refuse to yield to an alternate perspective? Did you ever feel like, what you think and say is completely invalidated. Well, at least that is how they make you feel.

One night I got together with two friends of mine. We had been pretty close for the past five years and we remain adult friends. We drank great wine and ate shrimp, steaks and potatoes from the grill. Jazz and acoustic rock coming from the radio. A chimenaya burned a Christmas wreath from the year before.

Casual conversation would lead into politics with an innocent comment about healthcare or social security and this day and age everything jumps directly to Iraq and George W Bush. My gracious host for the night contested that the World Trade Center collapsing was a controlled implosion and that Americans were maiming innocent three year olds in Iraq.

It sits uneasy with me. The liberal majority of the Mid-Atlantic. I tell myself at times I'd probably be better off in the plains or down in the south. It is so easy to push your hate and naiveté onto others with dissimilar beliefs. The minority may be right or maybe nobody is right but the minority is seldom, if not ever, judged as competent.

That night my two friends debated the maiming of three-year-old children in Iraq from bombs dropped by the US. They stated that casualties were astonishing and that within ten years our lives would see an apocalyptic catastrophe. That America funding and supporting the Israelis' was our downfall.

I troubled them to consider the onset of democracy, the development of new communities including schools and places of worship as well as the implementation of a free society. They dismissed this as "Outsourcing Democracy". A term I had never heard of before but one that I've thought about for quite some time.

There's always going to be a debate about what is right and what's wrong and that is what makes American's so arrogantly honest. I smoked cigarettes with my friends and they spoke of the desensitization of the American public considering the images and news of devastation. I countered the thought with our own domestic desensitization.

You only know what you here from a little box in your house. Each media outlet portrays their own agenda with self-relevance. I'm sorry to say that our conversation got heated as this topic normally does when debated but as refreshing as it is for me to hear another person's opinion I would assume it to be the same for my own audience.

In my life, I have always left myself open to criticism as well as opposing dialogue. I guess it's what make's me such a good salesperson. Sales 101 tells you that if you are talking then you are not selling. Listening is the key to selling. I never find myself talking end on end in one continuous run-on sentence of personal propaganda. I actually despise this sort of approach and wonder about people that can just talk for minutes on end.

Are some people really so self-absorbed that they actually believe that the thirty sentences they just connected and vocalized are so important that they needed to platform them without pause? Why talk without space for comment?

I think OJ Simpson was the first instance for me of true judicial failure. And the MOVE tragedy in Philadelphia was the first time I realized that not everything in the world was as it seemed. The Mayor at the time yielded all responsibility to the Police Commissioner to arrest the members of MOVE by any means necessary. I was nine years old.

The bomb dropped on the bunker of the West Philadelphia home sparked a fire destroying a community and a city. Since then, no Philadelphia police officer was fined, fired or suspended. However, the city was ordered to pay over $32 million to the casualties of the incident including 1.5 million to Ramona Africa and 29 million to the residents of Osage Avenue and Pine Streets.

The 29 million portion is still currently under appeal by then councilman and current mayor of Philadelphia, John Street. Yes, the same John Street who stood in line at the Promenade for an iPhone as *the city reached its 200ᵗʰ murder of the year in June of 2007.*

I remember bringing the MOVE newspaper headlines into school the next day for Current Events to talk about. I'd prepared to speak about what had happened and how it affected me. That day every other student brought in the same exact headline.

When I was eight years old I laid in my bed one night. I was awoken by the light of my door opening and saw the shadow of a man walking in. I lay still, unable to breathe. My throat dry. I pretended like I was sleeping as an intruder walked freely in my bedroom. Moments away from assault. The thirty seconds or so drug on like years.

The robber took my two dollars from atop my coin separator and walked out. Moments later I heard footsteps pounding as my father came down the stairs. There was someone in our home and he had just robbed us. The light from the living room shot on as my father bolted out the side door.

He chased the man straight down the road in his underwear. They found my mothers purse in the bushes of the side of the house. They found the thief at the dead end down the street. He was prosecuted and I testified in court against him.

I sat on the witness stand, eight years old. I described to the attorney how my two dollars were folded and my mother, who had just quit smoking, described the type of chewing gum she consumed. My two dollars were found folded and crumbled as I described and a Juicy Fruit wrapper was found in the crook's front pocket. He was sentenced to a few months in jail and taken away.

I had nightmares throughout the forthcoming months and had my first sense of anxiety as I felt he may come back to get me. He never did.

THE COURTS

They sat outside of the Municipal Building parking lot in an open space overlooking a softball field covered with fresh powder. The snow fell sideways and they could hear the whistle of the wind through the metal doors.

They talked for over an hour and weighed every realistic option between the five of them. Kelly must have apologized a dozen times before they got out and headed inside.

Behind the glass at the desk was an officer in uniform. He was all business and just looked up at them.

Hi officer. We need to speak to somebody about something that is going on. Mick said. Tonight we were shot at outside of Bailey's Bar and we really don't know where else to turn.

You were shot at? He pulled his brows up and his forehead wrinkled with suspicion. He leaned forward. What happened?

Well. We were outside of the bar and this guy jumped on our car and we sped away. He pulled a gun out and shot at us.

Now why would he do that?

I'll be honest with you. This is a very complex situation, which is going to need some confidential consultation.

Hmm. The officer reclined in his chair, which let out a squeal. Well. Why don't you wait right here and I'll get an officer on duty to speak with you.

In confidence. He got up and walked out of the reception area.

I can't believe this is happening. Olivia shuddered.

I'm sorry babe. I really am.

She didn't say a word. She looked out at the street and held Kelly's hair from her face.

The door opened to the waiting room and out came a plainclothes woman. She must have been in her late thirties with short brown hair. Her badge glistened off her belt next to the holstered Glock.

My name is Detective Sloane. Officer Rigsby tells me you're all in a bit of trouble and needed someone to talk to.

Yes. That's right. Mick stood up. We really need to talk about some things.

OK. Why don't you all come back with me and we can see what's going on. OK?

Mick looked at everybody one last time and agreed. They straggled in and down the hall. Sloane directed them into an interrogation room. This is the only room I got big enough for us all.

McKenzie immediately sat down at the table across from her.

So, what's going on?

We're in a lot of trouble ma'am. McKenzie said. Six months ago there was a rape in progress. Kelly winced and cried into Olivia's shoulders. My friend Kelly was being raped by these assholes. He motioned toward Kelly.

OK, son. Calm down. She leaned forward at the table.

It's all right Brad. Mick said.

I came out from the courts by the bridge and I heard her screaming. I went down the path and I came up on them. There was three of them. I shot one of them. He's dead. I killed him. They were raping her. She didn't ask for that.

I know, son. Was this the homicide under the turnpike bridge that you're talking about?

Yes. I did it. But they were raping her.

And there was two others?

Yes. And I've been living with this since then. Both of us have.

And somebody shot at you tonight in front of Bailey's?

Yes. Mick said.

Hold on. Just Brad right now. She interrupted.

Yes. It was him. I seen one of them in the bar and he saw me. We got out of there and got in the car. The Mexican jumped on the car and as we drove off he shot at us twice.

Who shot at you?

The black guy.

There were two of them?

Yes. Both of them from that night.

Can you describe them?

Yeah, the black guy looked like a bum. Dirty, unkept hair. Don't know, he looked like a bum. Tall. Real tall. The Mexican looked like Benicio Del Toro from Fear and Loathing in Las Vegas.

Sloane stood up. I'm gonna have to ask you all to stay here. She walked over to Kelly. Was it you? Kelly looked down in tears. I'm so sorry. Why didn't you ever say anything?

She looked even further down and away and couldn't muster up a syllable.

I understand. It's going to be all right. Just hang tight ok?

She closed the door behind her. Mick put his hand on his brother's shoulder. It's all right. Everything is going to be ok.

I'm going to jail aren't I?

No. The only place you're going is home.

Detective Sloane sat down at her desk and pulled up her computer screen to search the database for the record from that night. She called on the phone down to the tank. Hi Charlie. This is Detective Sloane. The two drunks you brought in tonight with the gun from Five Points. I'm gonna need you to bring them down for an ID.

She scanned the record, which was tagged as *UNSOLVED*. Pictures of the scene. Blood on the mattress. She read in the comment field; *Victim had been deceased for over 72 hours. Pants unbuckled with evidence of semen and pubic hair that which was not his own (Evidence Marked). Cause of Death: Multiple gunshots.*

The fluorescent light hummed in the interrogation room. They stood silent except for some sobs and words of salvation.

Guess nobody thought we'd end up here tonight? Pfifer tried to break the tension and it did for a second. Brad, Kelly. I want you both to know that I'm proud of you. And I'm behind you 100%. This is all going to work out. It has to. I mean we're all good people. We're not like them. Those assholes that did this to you. They have no right. It's all going to work out.

The click of the door handle being turned startled the lot of them. The door swung open and Sloane came in with a folder in her hand. She flicked a switch, which dimmed out the fluorescent light and lit up an orange one off on the distant wall.

OK. I'm going to need you three to sit over here please. And ma'am. I'm sorry, what is your name?

Kelly.

Kelly. Kelly, what is your last name?

Sanchez.

OK. Kelly. I need you to sit next to Brad. And at this point I'm going to have to advise you that this is a criminal investigation and anything you say can and will be used in a court of law. She took a deep breath. She pressed record on an old cassette player on the table. I'm going to bring two people into that room and I'm hoping we can get an ID on them.

In the room outside the window she could see a door open. The sound was muted and an officer led in two men handcuffed.

Now, I want you all to know. This is just like the movies. We can see them. They can't see us.

There were three officers and the two perps. The two men were shouting and being uncooperative with the cops. They stood them in the room for a good minute. And they got suspicious that something else was happening.

That's them. Both of them. With out question.

My god. Kelly said. That is them.

That is definitely the guys from tonight, Pfifer said.

We picked these two up at Five Points harassing some gas attendant. Turns out they were attempting to rob him and the one's got priors as long as a shopping list. The Puerto Rican I've never seen before, but the other one is cold-hearted. Sloane walked to the glass. What they did to you Kelly is a mortal sin. I'm gonna see to it that they never see the light of day again.

Kelly left about two hours after. They had her supply a sample of her blood and hair for evidence. She filled out a long form with her full account of the story. She took the pamphlets regarding counseling for women who have been involved in sex crimes and folded them into her front pocket.

Olivia drove her home in the dead of winter with Pfifer. Mick waited in the lobby for his brother. When they got to her house she told Kelly that if she needed anything at all to give her a call, you've got my number.

McKenzie spent that night at the police station. They questioned him for hours about his motive and what he had done. If he thought he used excessive force. He told them he did what he thought was right. They asked where the gun was and he said he tossed it in the Delaware.

In the weeks that passed more and more surfaced about the identity of the two men. They both came from broken homes and lived each day as it came. Tyrece James was the only man in his home. His father left them before he could remember and he lived with his mother and two younger sisters. He worked odd jobs for days until he got fired or quit from a lack of interest. He was 23 years old and sentenced to 20 years for First Degree Sexual Assault and an additional 5 for Conspiracy.

The Puerto-Rican, Jose Gonzalez was only sentenced for the conspiracy and got three years because of his clean prior record.

McKenzie never saw a day in court regarding the shooting, which was deemed necessary and justified, but he did get a hefty possession of weapons fine. His family sat in the courtroom with him, Mr. And Mrs. Sanchez and Kelly. She didn't even have to testify considering the overwhelming evidence. Jurors came back with a verdict within two hours.

When winter broke the campus hustled with excitement. Foliage whipped out from hibernation and blossoming trees lined the main street. Outside of The Smithson was a new banner advertising specials on Corona for $1.50 a bottle.

Chaps sat outside at a café table with Thunder tied to the wrought iron fence. He typed away at his laptop and sipped from a bottle of Mexican's finest with a lime. The breeze was as pleasant as the light traffic.

He wrenched under his shorts and tugged at a mosquito bite he had gotten from the woods the previous night. His face was already tan and his shoulders beamed under his loose muscle shirt. No freckles or unattended hair.

Lynn pounded outside with a tray full of drinks for a table full of girls on the other side of the entranceway. She dropped them off and came back over to Chaps.

Nice out today isn't it? She said.

Yes it is. A perfect day.

How long you plan on staying here?

Just about as long as my battery holds till I guess.

I guess you'll need another beer then, right?

Yeah, that'd be nice Lynn. He went on typing on the keyboard. Hits were up on the site and he had a business of his own. He employed a handful of folks to sell advertising and put together a monthly magazine on the area's entertainment scene.

He could see Travis coming down the main road from almost two blocks away. He hurried to bookmark some work and save files he would get to later. Once Travis got there it would be a whirlwind. He gave new meaning to time management.

Yo Chaps! He shouted from across the street. He jaywalked through the street. Chaps, how you doing? Chaps gave him a look and closed his laptop. Freakin' Beautiful day out today isn't it?

Yes it is. Travis hopped over the railing and pulled a seat over to his table. He plopped himself down beside him. I think we got a great start to the year coming.

Oh yeah?

Yes. Our funnel is full. He took his new role working for Chaps as Sales Manager seriously. Maybe too much so. The telemarketers he mentored really took a liking to him but Chaps could read through his bullshit like the Sunday comics.

That's good to hear. You're doing a great job, bud. You had a great closing to the year and I'm very proud of what you've been able to accomplish.

Thanks.

And not only the new job with my company but the sobriety and the total change in life thing that you've been doing.

Well, I guess it was time, ya know? There comes a point where you just gotta grow up. That day came when I had no trust fund coming in, no job and really no sense of purpose. I sat in front of my TV without anything to look forward to and I just said, I gotta make a change.

And you did that.

And here I am. I'm happier now.

Good. He gulped down the last of his beer and put the empty bottle down on the table in front of him.

The chattering laughter from the girls next to them built to an outrageous roar after a pounding thump, which drew their attention. Two of the young girls had slammed down their glasses while racing Long Island Iced Teas. They held their heads from the freeze inside their skulls.

Oh, to be young again. Lynn dropped off a beer for him. Nothing to worry about but getting to class on time.

Seriously. Chaps pondered about the café style seating and retreated in his company. Are you coming over to the house tonight?

Yeah, I'll be there after my shift. Like nine thirty.

OK.

Tell Mick I'll see him then.

All right.

Travis sucked down a diet coke and then caught a ride back to the house with Chaps. They drove through the hills just outside of the campus passing Old Victorian style homes with outstretched lawns.

The flatlands of the countryside and turning roads drifted them further and further out away from the town. They pulled up the street and the parking lot was already filled with cars. Two girls stumbled down the steep driveway holding hands toward their car.

Inside the bass was booming and all of the overheads had been switched with backlights and the large room was glowing. Chaps teeth shined bright white. They bumped through the crowd and funneled out of the kitchen into the backyard.

Off of the dirty porch sat Mick bare-chested in a

lawn chair with gold brimmed round sunglasses. His tie-dyed T-Shirt rested on the arm of the seat and his face was stretched toward the sun.

Wow, it's slamming with people already here. Chaps grabbed a beer from the cooler right next to his chair.

Yeah, I gotta stay out here.

Too many people?

Mick didn't say a word. The sun dropped quickly that night. It'd be no time before Pfifer showed up. They planned on driving straight threw to Pittsburgh to meet up with his brother. One last weekend road trip. Lynn made it to the house around nine thirty as she said she would and they spent maybe a half an hour together before the Jeep pulled up in the driveway.

Pfifer hit the horn to the secret pattern and Mick drew the shade open. They got out of bed and got dressed. He threw some half-clean clothes in a gym bag along with some deodorant and toothpaste. Down the hall he grabbed Travis who decided last minute he'd get out of town.

Lynn gave him a hug and kiss and the three of them were on their way. The Jeep backed down the drive in the pale of dusk. The streets were calm for a Friday night and they pushed the speedometer high above seventy.

Travis sat in the back seat rifling through a pair of pants he packed. He grabbed a vile out and immediately took a toot of the powder he had been hiding. Pfifer and Mick passed a blunt he had been saving for just this trip. Mick surfed his hand in the air of highway wind. He played the latest TOOL CD, which was so loud that nobody would be able to hear their cell phones.

They got to the Turnpike entrance ramp in no time and pressed on west. Outside of Pittsburgh they stopped along the shoulder and Travis went out in the woods.

You ready for this weekend? Pfifer asked.

Yeah.

You all right?

Yeah.

You just seem a little bit quiet.

What? I don't know.

It's gonna be fun.

Yeah, I know.

It was one in the morning by the time they pulled into the one-way street that McKenzie's row home was on. He sat out on the porch smoking a cigarette. Inside his roommates sat about in the living room space. They were all college seniors that were graduating that year. When he failed to return to classes in the beginning of the semester he moved from downtown to Oakland. Not the nicest section of town but many of Pitt, Duquesne and Carnegie Mellon students shacked up in the area so it was relatively a collegiate community.

The home at Edith Place was a two-story 2 bedroom 1 bath with an unfinished basement. McKenzie and his three roommates shared the $425 a month rent. He had been working odd jobs as a bike messenger and filling out surveys to pay the bills. The home was an artist convent for the most part. There were always people passing in and out.

One weekend in *the burgh* was filled with chemical experimentation, which lead to painting a Green Day CD cover across the entire living room wall. The adjacent wall had a mural of Jimi Hendrix. McKenzie shared a room with Stephen who was a self-proclaimed *alcoholic queer.*

The other room was Adam's; he was tiny in size but large in opinions. He was to graduate on the Dean's List and really had his act together. He had organized the house's lease and was also scheduling their eventual move to New York City. Lastly, down in the basement was Barb. Eccentrically eclectic and glamorous to boot. McKenzie had never ventured into the basement but often heard banging down there. She was top heavy and had full lips with a large smile. Her eyelashes were equally robust.

They'd often lay around the living room playing video games, smoking and talking about the state of the world. In the months together they'd grown into their own *true story, real world.* He did some work in local theatres to pass the time and played more guitar then he had ever played.

They came into the house and threw their bags on the floor in the front living room. They had a beer or two and crashed for the night.

In the morning they walked up Forbes Avenue and to The Cathedral to take a tour. Forty-Two stories above Pittsburgh they could see the rivers that surrounded the city and all the way out past the mountains. The roommates shared most of the day with them.

They spent most of the day doing the tourist thing and then met up with Kelly and Simpson at the Playhouse. The two of them didn't hit it off as a couple but remained friends that semester. Kelly never really got over the feeling of a man's touch on her body and was unable to trust him in any other role.

They got to the Ticket Booth and used Adam's college ID card to get free passes for the performance of HAIR that Stephen was in. He played Berger, the second lead in the show. In true sixties fashion they smoked up before, during and after the show. It was a non-nude performance in a black box stage.

After the show they mingled about and heard of a cast party in Oakland. A block down the road from Edith Place. They walked down the main road, stopping only at a local convenience store for a quick dinner.

The clerk was a friend of McKenzie's and he always let him take what ever he wanted, no questions asked. The whole crew loaded up on Ben & Jerry's ice cream, all beef hot dogs and sodas. He didn't own the place. He just worked there and could care less.

They got back to the house and settled in the living room around the TV. Stephen went upstairs to take off the rest of his stage makeup and get dressed. He took a liking to Travis and offered him a quick bump of heroin, which he accepted.

I don't get that, Mick said.

What's that? Pfifer asked.

Well, he tells Chaps that he's all clean and sober and then the moment he gets in the car with us he's doing that shit. He's drinking and now he's gonna snort heroin?

Some things never change I guess.

He's always been that way, since I first met him.

Want to hear that song? McKenzie prompted.

Yeah. Let's hear it. He went upstairs to get his guitar and knocked on the locked door. Stephen opened the door in just a towel wrapped around the lower section of his body. Travis sat on the edge of McKenzie's bed.

I just want to get my guitar. Why you locking the door? He crossed the room and picked up the Samick guitar from its stand. It was a blonde guitar with a chipped pick guard. It had several local band stickers on it. He had bought it when he was back home for just over a hundred dollars. The action was awful and the strings on it were mostly black from the dirt on his fingers.

Still it was an impressive instrument, which he loved the feel and smell of. Heavy wood and warm acoustic tones.

He could play open chords. Mainly rhythm guitar and learned some structure and theory. He wrote folk rock songs and sang with a twang.

He cradled the guitar in his arms and walked out of the room. When he came down the stairs he heard the sounds of Street Fighter coming from the video game system. Pfifer and Adam were glued to the TV while Kelly, Barb and Mick laid back on the couch. He sat down in the papa son chair and strummed a few chords.

Travis came down moments later and his eyes were already distant. He was quiet and sunk into the love seat. By the time Stephen came down the steps they were already high. They asked each other if they *feel it* and Travis said his face was melting off. They wandered around the house aimlessly until Adam guided them out the front door. Travis fell down the porch steps onto the broken concrete sidewalk. It was the first wound of the night with many more to follow.

Kelly and McKenzie walked side by side down the one-way alley of row homes. They fell behind the others, just beneath their stretching shadows that lay before them.

Would you ever shoot heroin? She asked him.

No. Never. I don't think that I would. I think I'd lose my mind or my heart would blow up.

I wouldn't either.

I'll smoke weed and drink beer, that's about it. Nothing more.

That's smart.

Even the weed anymore. I'm pretty much done with it. I get paranoid and I don't like that feeling.

Stick to the beer.

Yeah. He laughed at her sense of humor, which always made him feel at ease. They walked up to the brick faced home and could see a full house of people through the front two windows. They heard the radio playing a soundtrack from a musical.

Sounded like a big show-tune finale. Pfifer looked at McKenzie with a smirk.

What are we getting ourselves into here?

Relax, said McKenzie. Just open your mind to the unknown. Worst case, you may see some guys kissing, or a drag queen. They're harmless though.

The rickety screen door opened and the sounds rushed out into the street. At the door was Fannon, an over the top African-American homosexual with a half shirt on.

Hello, come on in all. He shouted with a large smile. Mick recognized him from the show they saw earlier that night and complimented him on his performance.

Thank you so much. He leaned out of the door and gave Mick a big hug. Mick thought it was a big laugh and played along. Hello Stephen. Hello? Earth to Stephen? Stephen was pale and empty and the skin under his eyes dragged to the ground. He mustered enough steam to part his lips and mutter nothing more then breath. He raised his hand and grabbed the screen door and stumbled into the house. My, my. Looks like the Stephen we all know and love. Travis walked straight by him and stuck to Stephen tightly.

Hi Fannon, Kelly said. She gave him a kiss on each cheek.

Hello darling. Hi McKenzie. He gave a seducing look at McKenzie and Pfifer as they passed in the home.

Inside there were players from the show they had just seen which Mick got a kick out of. Seeing them in their show, then out of costume and talking to all of them. The one female lead held her lips to a five-foot water bong as someone crouched down on the ground and lit it for her.

They settled into the back den, which overlooked a courtyard through large pane glass windows. Outside there was a floodlight that lit the foliage of the garden. It was a peaceful space.

Travis plopped down on the love seat next to Kelly and leaned on her arm and shoulder. He rested his head on her neck and she could all but feel his saliva dripping on her.

Do you want to go out back and fuck? He put his arm on her lap and squeezed her.

She shuffled over to the arm of the couch and screamed. Fuck you, you asshole.

She stood up and looked back down on him. She kicked at his shin with her sandals with sharp force. Three times she kicked him then she jumped down on him and hit him in the face with an open palm strike.

She wailed with both arms maybe ten times before McKenzie and Pfifer even got close to them. She screamed at him and she was crying. Travis all but lay there and lift his arms to protect his face.

When they pulled her off of him his face was scratched and bleeding. Her hair had been rummaged and her shirt was askew. You're a fucking asshole, she screamed and walked out the back of the house.

McKenzie went outside behind her and comforted her. What happened?

You don't want to know what he said to me. She collected herself in the courtyard. Do you have a cigarette?

He reached into his front pocket and gave it to her. She took the lighter from him and struck it with her shaking fingers several times. Fucking lighter. She could only get a spark from it.

Here, hang on. Let me do it.

No fuck you Brad. She screamed and paced about the pavers. She grunted with frustration and finally got a flame to her cigarette. You can't always be helping me, you know. You're not always going to be able to protect me. I mean, godammit. What a complete jerk he is. I should have killed him.

You did a pretty good job in there on him.

He deserves a limb to be severed.

Come on, he's high Kelly.

He's high? She laughed. That's no fucking excuse, she continued. He's high? What, does that give him free reign on the English vocabulary? Does that mean that he can touch me and grope me and say what ever the fuck he wants? Because he's high? No, that's bullshit Brad. His ignorance doesn't mean that I should suffer humiliation and shit, man. It boggles my mind that there are these complete assholes out there with no respect for women or really any respect for themselves. That he can come on to me completely out of the blue and I'm supposed to just dismiss it and think of it only as 'some dumb fuck being high'. The feeling I have knowing that some jerk is thinking about me that way is absolute disgust. And for you to rationalize it with your fucking, 'he's high' is an insult to me and I hate you for it. Were you raped Brad? Did you have somebody force himself into you? No.

You weren't. You don't know anything about what I feel. I have to live with that for the rest of my life. Some dick forced himself into me and ripped my skin. Punched my face and took away all of me. You don't know anything about what I feel.

Kelly. I'm sorry.

I'm going home Brad. She ran out under the arbor and back to the alley. Mick opened the back door and poked his head out.

Everything all right out here?

No.

Todd Bailey

THE COURTS

VIII

O ver the summer McKenzie spent most of his time going to Open Mics and writing songs with his roommates. Olivia rented a studio apartment up the road. They picnicked in the park and she worked at an Ice Cream shop for cash.

McKenzie kept to his ubiquitous ways. Donating plasma, working children's theatre, waiting tables and performing on the sidewalks with his guitar case open.

Sunday evenings were spent on the hill at the park where they watched free movies outdoors. Olivia enjoyed the attention and the two became inseparable.

He didn't see much of Kelly that summer. A few times at the Playhouse. Just casual greetings. Closed mouth smiles. An occasional conversation.

When fall finally came around and classes started up again he was left alone to come to grips with his decisions. He needed to find a place for himself in this life and it wasn't going to be in Pittsburgh, PA.

He sold his mountain bike and stereo system. He took out as much cash as he could against his credit cards and bank account and came up with over eight hundred dollars cash. He wrote one last bad check for a bus ticket to Hollywood, California.

If ever there was a time to give it a run it was now. The night before he left town his roommates threw him a big party at the house. Olivia came and brought him a card to wish him well. That night they slept together in uncertainty.

In the morning she went with him to the bus station. He packed everything he could in a garbage bag and his army bag. They sat at the station in stationary plastic seats holding hands. He told her he loved her several times and rubbed her forearms gently.

When the bus came he packed his things in one of the storage compartments and got on. He watched her from the window as she walked away. It would take almost three days to make the trip by Greyhound. There is a lot of time to think crossing the country.

He had just left everything behind. Security. Family. Love. He hadn't even called home to tell his parents. Last he heard from them was a phone call telling him that Mick was transferring to a bigger Division I college in Missouri or Massachusetts. He hadn't even gotten the details other then there was a falling out with the coaches.

He heard there was a knife fight with Travis at the converted Firehouse apartment and Chaps fired him. Things got so bad for Travis that he ended up having to be shipped back home and go into rehab.

He thought a lot about his brother. How he would do this year. He took comfort knowing that whatever he did it would make him proud. And he knew the same was true for him. He'd use the calling card Olivia gave him and give him a call when he got to Hollywood. Surprise him.

The bus stopped one morning in the middle of the desert at a truck stop. He went into the gift shop and walked around. Got some breakfast and went to the bathroom. When he came out the bus was gone. He got real scared for a minute. There was nobody around. No one he knew. He cursed himself, then the bus driver.

Back inside he questioned the clerk at the counter who laughed mercilessly and told him he wasn't the first person to be left out here by a bus and that another one would be around in six hours or so. He never felt so insignificant in his life.

Then he worried about his bags and his guitar and the clerk told him to call the eight hundred number on his ticket to report the incident, which he did. The customer service rep on the phone assured him that his belongings would be waiting for him when he arrived.

The next bus came about four hours later and he got on without any issue. He got into Nevada in his third day on the road. He hadn't showered since Pittsburgh and was clammy. It was nighttime when they passed Las Vegas and the lights shined bright. It reminded him of Atlantic City, how he would drive the expressway to the parkway and see the hotels. This was much more beautiful to him though.

Memories of his visit to Vegas rushed him. He was twelve or thirteen and he and his brother wrestled in a tournament out there. They stayed at Circus Circus. It was the first time he ever saw his parents truly kiss. One night when walking to the hotel from a restaurant or a tourist attraction they crossed a parking lot and his father planted one on his mother.

The McKenzie brothers looked at each other and made faces of disgust. Not something you really need to see as a child, as innocent as it was. It was nice to think that his parents got along so pleasantly.

It was early morning when they came into Los Angeles. The sky was orange, thick with the most muggy air he had seen. Smog was something he had heard of, this was even fouler then he had imagined.

When he stepped off the bus he thought of Neil Armstrong's *One Small Step for Man, One Giant Leap for Mankind* saying and smirked. He promised himself to become famous, to make a name for himself and to not disappoint.

His bags and guitar were waiting for him by the ticket booth and he picked them up quickly. Outside he sat at a bench and opened a map he had printed out the night before he left Pittsburgh. He lit a cigarette and smoked quietly in LA.

Once his bearings were set he went to the taxi stand and told the cabbie to take him to the youth hostile on Cahuenga.

Where you from?

Philly.

Oh yeah? What brings you to LA?

I'm an actor. I'm gonna give it a run.

Oh, ok. What do you think so far?

What do you mean?

What do you think of Los Angeles?

It's cute.

Cute? I never heard the city described as cute before. He looked out the window and wondered about the unfamiliar town. If it was just digital data that god created each and every day of his life and that maybe he had been making him work over time to create this scene. He thought about how weird a thought that was and smiled again. He was finally there.

He got out of the cab at the hostel and checked in. It was a quaint room with a nice full size bed. He dropped his bags off and walked down to Hollywood Boulevard to see what that was all about. There it was. The stars on the street. Mann Chinese Theatre and the wax museum.

He ate lunch at McDonalds and grabbed a free apartment guide. He walked the streets off the boulevard going in and out of property manager's offices asking the rents. Finally he found one for $395 a month and they accepted his application. Probably didn't even look at it. It was on Yucca, one block off the boulevard. No security deposit. It wasn't too bad either. Studio, bathroom, shower and kitchen.

He ignored the large banner that was strung across the entrance of the street that read *Street under continuous surveillance for gang activity.*

He walked back up the hill toward the Hollywood Bowl and went into his room at the hostile. He packed up his things, checked out of the hostile and got most of his money back. It was a good mile walk with all of his gear.

Inside of the apartment he set up a mock sleeping area and unfolded all of his clothes against the bare wall. Outside the window he could see the in ground pool in the courtyard and thought he might take a swim later. He laid down and stared at the ceiling. He tried to shut his eyes and sleep but couldn't. He locked the door behind him and set out to explore. He found a pay phone down the road and wrote down the number on it. He sorted through the attached phone book and then picked up the receiver.

When the voice on the other end answered it had been a good two minutes used on his card. It was the phone company and he scheduled new service but they wouldn't be out for three days at least. He hung up and went down to the boulevard and walked the street all the way down to West Hollywood. He took note of places that he would come back to. He'd need a job. When it got dark out he headed back home and slept until the next afternoon.

THE COURTS

He sat on the curb of Hollywood Boulevard with his thinly stretched hand open. His corduroys had been torn at the cuffs and his sweater had threads pealing from the collar. Passerby's paid him no mind at all. He hadn't spoken to anybody but himself in almost a month. Funny how the mind shoots in all directions without social stimulation. He was scattered.

Two nights ago was Thursday. That was the last time he ate. A community outreach had shut the doors at McDonalds and let in homeless people for a cheeseburger, fries and a soda. It wasn't much but it got him by until tonight. He thought about not even going in for the food. That he was admitting to himself that he was in trouble but he was too hungry.

He couldn't get work. Couldn't even get a phone call in the two months before the phone got disconnected. He hadn't had more then five dollars in his pocket for quite some time. Once he got thrown out of the apartment complex he hid his things and his guitar behind the dumpster at the Mann Chinese Theatre. Occasionally he sat outside strumming with the case open and that got him by the day to day.

The stores had been closed for a good while. He sat in front of the metal sliding door that slid down to protect the glass window from vandals. Across the street he saw a family of punks that he passed by many times. It was a guy and a girl with a little boy and a dog. They seemed in such good spirits for not having a home and it being forty degrees out.

He couldn't take much more of this. He couldn't survive on half eaten food from trashcans and the ground. It was wrong and he shouldn't be there. He was filled with hate and frustration. He was tired.

From the side of the road he could see a white van pull up. It stopped right in front of him. On the passenger door there was a graphic of a dove and a hand in a house, printed in royal blue. The passenger window rolled down from the driver leaning across the seat. He was a large black man with a gentle smile.

Hey, did you need some help?

McKenzie stared in complete submission. He was smart enough to know who he was and what the van meant. He had seen it stopping by on countless nights before. One by one picking up kids on the street. He was a volunteer from The Covenant House, which was a non-profit shelter for homeless, runaway and throwaway youth. He thought about sticking it out on the street one more night and maybe someone would call him at the payphone with a job. He thought maybe he could panhandle with his guitar in the morning.

Maybe I'll just find out a little bit about what you're all about? He got up off the street and came over to the van. The man explained about the program. That they weren't just a shelter or Crisis Center but that they had a full program to get kids back on their feet. Set them up with job opportunities and more. He told him that if he was in trouble he could always call the nine line at 1-800-999-9999 and they were there to help.

The man got out of the van and came around onto the sidewalk. He shook his hand and introduced himself as Reggie, a previous runaway. He was about six foot five inches and almost three hundred pounds at first glance. McKenzie told him about where he came from and how he got there and how he couldn't get a job. Reggie said he heard it all before and that he wasn't alone. The important thing was to get him off the street. It had been months of solitaire. It had been months of struggle.

He helped carry his things from behind the theatre and loaded up the van. They drove up the street and turned down Western Avenue. They pulled into the complex just before midnight and he went through sort of a pre-registration interview. They made him call his parents. It was the first time he spoke to his father since he arrived six months ago. He heard his mother crying in the background but he could also hear the relief in his father's voice.

He spent four months in the program, got a job working as an office clerk at an AIDS Hospice and moved back out on his own. He moved into a small apartment back on Yucca St and made ends meet. Every other week he collected a check that covered the rent and food.

He got a call from home telling him that his sister's wedding was coming up and that his father had gotten him a plane ticket home.

You're welcome to stay home too. You don't have to go back to LA, his father said.

McKenzie took comfort in that. He spent the next two weeks exploring the city. He went to the Santa Monica Pier and Venice Beach. Did the tourist thing. He visited an Uncle that lived in Venice. In a bungalow near where Jim Morrison resided. He took him on a tour of his guitar shop where he made custom guitars. He touched his feet in the Pacific Ocean.

Kelly drew the shades of her apartment closed. She smelled the scent of the candles that she blew out moments ago. She turned the Counting Crows CD playing on the boom box off and picked up her keys. Her purse was unusually heavy from the steel inside. She locked the door behind her and wheeled her suitcase to the cab on the street. She took one last look at the playhouse as she drove by. The streets of Pittsburgh were always clean. The crystals on the sidewalk shimmered as they passed.

She got to the Bus station for the drive home. It was Spring Break and there were other college kids getting on the bus. She took a window seat in the middle of the bus and the seat next to her remained empty for the entire five-hour drive to Levittown. The bus took to the turnpike quickly and rode the right lane for the most part. They pulled in at two rest stops along the way but made good time.

When she arrived in the shopping center and got off the bus her mother was waiting. She clapped and smiled as she got off the bus. Kelly drew a blank smile and accepted her hug. Mrs. Sanchez stroked the back of her head.

Oh, I missed you so much, she said. How are you?

I'm tired. Long drive.

Oh my baby. She shook her back and forth. Well, let's get your stuff. They packed her bags in the trunk and drove off. Kelly kept her eyes out the passenger window most of the ride.

How's school going?

It's OK.

And the audition?

I got the part.

That's great honey! But, you don't seem excited.

Yeah, I am. I'm just tired mom.

Is everything all right?

Yeah.

Todd Bailey

THE COURTS

IX

McKenzie spent the last of the forty dollars he had on a soda and the taxi ride to LAX. He never turned the key in to the apartment landlord. He told Reggie, whom he'd kept in touch with that he'd see him in a week and he packed as much as he could in a garbage bag and the green army backpack. He left his other hand open to carry the Samick guitar.

The cab pulled up and the driver opened the trunk. He pulled off Yucca St. for a final pass down Hollywood Boulevard. He hadn't made it big as a star but he had survived in a more meaningful journey.

Traffic was heavy and it took him an hour to get through US-101 and the interstate. The city spread out before him and he promised himself he'd be back for round two.

He checked his bags in and made it up to the gate. He carried his guitar with him and brushed his long stringy hair over his ears. His favorite sweater had a hole at the cuff by this point and the thread was still pulling. His green corduroys hung over his sneakers so much that he stepped on them in the back. He had experienced the west coast and all of its lack of opportunity. The city was mean to him and he would never forgive it.

The plane flew over the Hoover Dam and he looked out over it from the window. He sat in coach and slept a good portion of the flight. This trip would be almost twenty times shorter then the trip out months ago. His mind treated him to thoughts of old friends.

What Pfifer was up to. If his parents would both be there when he came up the ramp. If his mother would cry. If she was OK. If his brother was home yet and what his sister's new husband would be like once he really go to know him. God, getting married. That's like so over the top, he thought.

There was a layover in St. Louis for two hours. He just sat at the gate. He had been to St. Louis as a kid and gone up the Arch in its elevator. It was a Fourth of July weekend and there was a beer festival going on. There was what seemed like a million people spread out below him and they looked like ants from atop the *Gateway to the West*.

Still, this trip was melancholy. He never felt like more of a failure. He had lost his scholarship and dropped out of college, packed up everything and moved 2500 miles across the country. Wanting so badly to make his family proud by becoming something but not even coming close. It was human failure at its rotten core.

When he came up the ramp in Philadelphia he saw both his Mom and Dad waiting. An overwhelming sense of disappointment hit him and it was *he* that cried. His dad squeezed him so tight he heard his back crack and he gasped.

Oh god. I'm so glad you're home, he said. You're so thin.

I love you both.

His mother hugged him.

I don't want to go back dad.

OK, son.

I know I told you to get me the roundtrip ticket, but I can't go back.

It's OK. Don't worry about it. I'm just glad you're home.

You need a haircut and new clothes, his mother said. He laughed. They all laughed. They walked up the open hall past the gates and down to baggage. All the while Mr. McKenzie kept a tight grasp around his shoulders. They walked awkwardly but McKenzie could care less. He knew he would eat well, have money and clothes and most importantly the love from his family that he had not had since he left for college almost two years ago.

Is Mick home? He asked.

No not yet. He gets in tomorrow.

How's he doing.

Well, OK. He's having some tough times but he'll pull through just fine. We'll see him when he gets home. We'll cook up a nice spaghetti dinner and we'll all talk about what we've been doing.

McKenzie told them some stories of the places he had been, The Griffin Observatory where they filmed *Rebel Without a Cause*, NBC studios that he took a tour of, Venice Beach and the Santa Monica Pier. He told them he was excited to see Olivia again. That he loved her and missed her. He grabbed the garbage bag from the baggage claim and his mother gasped.

Oh my god, she said. You fit everything you have in that bag?

Most of it. I left some things behind.

We'll have your Uncle get them and ship them back. They grabbed a cart for the bags and walked out into the parking terminal. He popped the trunk to the Sebring and tossed in his gear.

The trip up I-95 was peaceful. He had survived an adventure of mass proportion. Not even twenty-one years old and he had given it a shot. Past the graffiti tags and tire graveyards of the city are the most stunning murals in the world. Hand painted dreams placed on top of brick and mortar. Off Second and Callowhill was an impressive piece that outlined the constitution and presidents of the United States and it was his favorite. He always made a point when he had passed it as a kid to take notice.

They got to the Bristol exit in no time at all. It was still light out and his dad took him past the High School into Indian Creek. His house looked exactly the same as when he had left. The crap rats across the street had added a new collection of lampposts and a garden swing that was rusted and falling apart.

Some things never change.

That's the beauty of it, son. He pulled up the cracked driveway and yanked the parking brake on.

They got out and he dragged his bags into his room.

Make sure you make a couple piles, whites, darks and towels and I'll get to it tonight. His mother said.

OK. He laid the bag on the floor and stood for a moment looking at the room. It was spotless. His trophies were on the same shelf, untouched. His posters were there. The calendar from two years ago was still on September. He closed the door leaving just a crack and sat on the edge of his waterbed. His emotions came over him and he cried again. His dad came in the room to talk and saw him.

Hey. He sat down next to him. You're OK. He grabbed his head.

I know. I'm just glad to be home.

I know. I'm glad you're home. We both are.

I'm so sorry. I feel like such a failure.

You're not. A failure would have never come back. In life, it's always OK to ask for help. The most important thing you have is your family. Never forget that.

That night Olivia came into town for the wedding. Mr. McKenzie cooked his award winning Veal Birds and Dub Dubs. They shared stories of their time at college and she went on and on about the state college she had transferred to and how she loved living back at home, how much happier she was. She helped clean up the dishes with Mrs. McKenzie before they went out for a night on the town. They shopped on South Street and he bought her a crazy outfit from Zipperhead that she liked and could wear the next day.

It was a crisp night and they went down to Penn's Landing on the Delaware River. They sat on a bench and looked out at glorious Camden, NJ. They kissed a bit and talked about the time that had passed. It was nice for him to be back in the arms of someone he loved. They drove home and she spent the night in his room.

Mick drove the turnpike straight through and got in by ten in the morning. He stopped the car on the grass between the sidewalk and the street and turned off the radio. The door squealed open and he dropped his feet to the pavement.

Home sweet home. He came straight up to the house. Hello? I'm home.

Brad could hear from his bed. He lay still with Olivia under his arm. His mother was excited and laughed when she saw him.

Oh, I'm so glad your home, she said.

His room had been converted to a den and had a pull out bed that came from under the couch. Mr. McKenzie had built a trophy rack that ran the length of the room and still had the dust on each award. It was good luck not to dust them.

The smell of scrapple & bacon came into his bedroom and they got out of bed. Olivia threw on some tight sweat shorts and a top and came out with Brad. Hey Mick, he said. Good to see you.

Hey brother. Hello Olivia.

Hi.

Good to see you.

Like wise, welcome home. She held onto Brad's side for security.

Now, you guys have to go and get fitted for your tuxedos and meet up for the rehearsal at the church by six o'clock. His mother was a stickler for organization and the boys had grown up on lists and regiment. Let's have some breakfast.

Jeez mom, let him get in the door first. She went out to the diningroom. What's going on? McKenzie was eager to catch up with his brother and it was the longest amount of time they had ever been apart.

Not much. She's getting married. Can you believe it?

Yeah, it's crazy.

After breakfast they took the Excel up to Bidwell's barber Shop and got a cut for $12 each. They went to the mall and got fitted at the tux shop. The whole mall had been remodeled and looked nothing like they remembered. Olivia basked in the attention of the two boys. They spent the day shopping then going to Pfifer's to catch up.

They sat in his apartment with a hockey game on the TV and vegged out. Pfifer was the same old bachelor that they had remembered. High in spirit. He had a new roommate and some new friends that were there as well. It was as if he hadn't missed a beat.

It was almost five o'clock when the phone rang. Pfifer answered the phone.

Hello. McKenzie could see him across the room. Yeah, he's right here. It's your mom. McKenzie got up from the couch and stepped over the coffee table to the kitchen. He rubbed his newly cut hair and took the phone. Hello? What? He raised his voice in terror. Oh my god. Most everyone in the apartment got quiet. Oh no. His eyes teered up and he turned away to the kitchen. No. Oh my god. No. There was some time that he stood with the phone clutched at his ear. He had his chin tucked down.

What's going on? Mick asked.

I don't know, said Pfifer. It was your mom. She said she needed to talk to Brad and it was important.

Ok. I love you. He hung up the phone. Kelly's dead. She killed herself. She's dead.

Oh my god. What happened. Pfifer got up and came into the kitchen and grabbed him.

I don't know. She killed herself last night. She's dead. Her mother called and told mom. The funeral is on Sunday. I don't know what to do. Pfifer hugged him tight and Mick came over. Olivia was by his side.

I'm so sorry. She said. They stood in the kitchen sobbing in disbelief. McKenzie trembled and moaned in a state of shock.

I don't know what to do. I can't stand this.

The drive to the church was quiet. Olivia sat in the back seat and talked about the things she remembered about her. The first time they met in the dorms and the crazy drawings she had done that she loved. McKenzie was exhausted from the emotional outpour by the end of the fifteen-minute drive.

Outside the church his parents waited by their car. The boys pulled into a spot near by and climbed out. Olivia came around and grabbed McKenzie. She all but held up his limp body as they walked toward the church.

I'm so sorry, his father said. She was a great friend. What happened?

Her mother called and said she took her life yesterday. She wanted you to know because she knows how close you two are. She was very sad. This whole situation is very sad. I'm so sorry for you.

I can't believe this.

I know. This is really a shock, his father said.

The funeral is going to be on Sunday. I know this is difficult for you and it's going to take some time to heal. Your father and I are here for you. You understand? His mother held her fingers against her lips and her eyes were wide.

Yes.

They came into the church and canned their emotions for the night. A miracle was shown in front of them. How life continues on. The McKenzie's daughter was glowing with joy. There were maybe thirty close guests that were present and the priest organized the rehearsal.

The McKenzie brothers practiced their ushering and the walk down the aisle and the positioning for the altar.

They followed the rehearsal with a reception at a local Italian restaurant. His sister came over and told him she was sorry to hear what had happened and that she was glad that he was there for her wedding. It was brilliant for him to connect with her again.

Anthony was tall and handsome. His thick mustache was well groomed. Not what he would have pictured for a brother in law but he went out of his way to make certain everyone was comfortable. Anthony's family was skeptical of the Irish-Italian relationship and made certain it was known. His family kept to themselves at their table and spoke Sicilian. It was like a scene out of a movie. Olivia and the brothers thought it was surreal and had a good time with the whole thing.

The crushing thunder sounded as if it were right outside his first story window. He had been awake for a half an hour now. Lying on the bed staring at his alarm clock. It was 6:42 AM. Another lightning struck. The thunder right after. Less then a mile away.

The rain pounded off the pane glass and it felt like it was thumbing on his head. He shuffled in the bed.

Can't sleep? Olivia whispered in a raspy tone.

No. She grabbed his hair and rubbed it.

Me neither.

He turned around and faced her. He could see a shadow cast down on her cheek and enough light was out that he could tell her eyes were a pale shade of blue. He rubbed his fingers over her shoulder.

Why did she have to do this?

I don't know. Some things in life we will never know. It must have been what she wanted. Do you think it's cowardly?

No. I used to think that about suicide, but now I don't know. The weight on his chest was immense. He turned his head and looked up at the window. Another lightning crashed down. Damn it's raining out there. I always thought that suicide was just outright giving up on life. Now that I know somebody that has done it, I just don't know. I guess I need time to let it soak in.

Yeah. It's really sad, she said. It's going to be a sad day.

They got out of bed and went in to the kitchen and made coffee. Olivia poured extra cinnamon in his because she new he liked it that way. Even the coffee mugs were shaped like owls. It was eerie. They sat on the screened three-season patio out back and watched the rain bounce off the basketball court in his backyard. He cried some more and she held him tight.

Hey, how you kids doing? Mr. McKenzie said from the doorway.

I'm sad dad. I'm just really sad. He sat down with them.

I know son. This is very difficult. It's going to be a tough day for you both. You've got to keep your head up and be strong though. It's not you OK. She loved you very much and whatever made her. Whatever was going on that made it too difficult for her to go on must have been something truly terrible. And I'm sure she is in a better place now.

Thanks dad.

Sure thing. I'm gonna get some coffee. Go pay your respects today. Say your good-byes. Get some closure. It'll be good for you.

Your dad is a good man, ya know.

Yeah, he's the best.

As morning ended they headed off to the mall again to get Olivia a dress to wear. They stopped for lunch at a fast food joint and sat almost paralyzed in the booth. Not much conversation. He felt like a zombie.

They got to Macy's and she tried on a few black dresses. They all looked great on her body and he couldn't help her choose. She picked the one she thought was the most tasteful and wore it out of the store. McKenzie bought two umbrellas and a pair of black sunglasses.

They got to the funeral home and there was a good number of people he remembered from High School. He spotted Angie immediately and wondered why she would come. Today was not the day to even acknowledge her. He walked past her, tilted his umbrella a bit to shield his view of her and walked on by. Olivia by his side. He didn't say a word. They got inside and there was a poster board of pictures from her life.

They walked down the long aisle and approached the closed casket. There was a beautiful 8" x 10" picture of her in a gold frame that sat next to some lilies that draped over the casket. He bowed his head and prayed for forgiveness. He prayed that she be let into heaven. It wasn't her fault, he said. He squeezed his eyes as tight as he could and grabbed his forehead until he could get a picture of her in his mind.

They sat down in the midst of many people. A priest said some words and her cousin read a eulogy. They played some of her favorite music from CD's and he cried uncontrollably. Olivia was crying and they held each other's hands tightly. He wiped his eyes and nose with a Kleenex that ripped in the stubble on his face.

The funeral procession was a fifteen-minute drive in the downpour. The windshield wipers splashed the rain from side to side. They got to the cemetery and they had a short walk to the plot. They stood together under the umbrellas. His shoes were full of mud. Ashes to ashes, dust to dust. He poured some dirt on the casket and walked to the car. He met up with some of her family and they invited them to come over for food and drinks.

They pulled along side the curb of the house off Radcliffe Street. They opened their umbrellas and raced up to the front door. He never knew that she had a relative that lived so close, let alone in this house. It was a large three-story, single family that backed up to the Delaware River. Inside was her mom.

Hi Brad, she said. She came over and hugged him. He sobbed into her shoulder.

I'm so sorry Mrs. Sanchez.

I know Brad. It's OK. She's in a better place now. She really loved you. You were a good friend. Now, don't be a stranger to me OK? I want to know when you are doing plays or what you are writing. She would want me to know.

OK.

Promise me Brad.

I promise.

They sat a while out back on the deck and looked out at the water. Mr. Sanchez came outside and walked to him. His suit had rain spots on it and his hair was wet. His eyes were deep and lost. He got close to McKenzie and he looked up at him.

Hi Brad.

Hi Mr. Sanchez. He knew him enough to say hello and that was about it. She had always talked about him and how they had some issues at home. He got on her case about grades and staying out late. High School stuff.

Can you walk with me son?

Sure. He got up and they walked down the steps out into the backyard. They crossed the grass and then down to a long straight wooden pier. They walked out and stopped at the end. They were a good thirty feet off shore. There were no boats on either side. He leaned on the railing and looked out. McKenzie followed.

I miss her Brad. Very much so. My heart is empty. I keep running it through my mind. The last time I saw her. Now here we are. I just buried my only daughter. Where would she get a gun?

His heart dropped and he wondered how it had happened. He hadn't even questioned in his mind the actual act.

She shot herself?

You didn't know?

No. I didn't want to think about it actually.

Yeah. She used a handgun and shot herself in the side of her head.

His head spun again in vertigo and he grabbed the rotted wood railing for support. Oh my god. He vomited off the side of the pier into the river.

Are you all right? He leaned over spitting into the brown water. He looked at his reflection and wondered if it was his gun.

No, I don't feel too good. I'm sorry.

I know, it's very tough.

I'm so sorry Mr. Sanchez.

We all are Brad. She wanted you to read this. It's the note she left when we found her body. His words up between the high-pitched sounds of emotion and tears. He pulled out a photocopy of the note from the inside pocket of his jacket. It was a folded piece of paper. He turned to him and took it. Don't read it now. Please.

Mr. Sanchez rapped his arms around him and fisted the shoulders of his jacket. He squeezed him so hard it pulled McKenzie's shirt out of his pants. He pulled back, looked him in the eye and rubbed his head. Now you make the best of your life, OK? Take each moment and cherish it. You only go around once so be nice to people. Tell your parents you love them as much as possible and never give up. OK?

McKenzie shook his head and looked down at the note. Mr. Sanchez walked back up the long pier and he watched him for a while.

They said their good-byes to the family and some of his old high school friends. On the way back home McKenzie told Olivia to make a quick stop. They turned down the road he had spent much of his elder teen years on. The tall trees were in full bloom, the rain had all but stopped and it was all too familiar for him.

He took her down past Angie's house. He didn't mention it to her as they passed. No reason to. He directed her into an empty parking lot and had her park the car. They sat in the car looking at an empty basketball court.

Are you OK? Olivia turned the car off and looked at him. They were drained of tears, lost from innocence but together. She touched his hand, which laid on his thigh. Brad?

Can we get out for a minute? He opened the car door and walked up to the bleachers. She followed behind and they sat on the bottom row. She left a note. Her dad gave it to me. She wanted me to see it. He pulled the paper from his pocket and held it in from of him still folded.

I'm afraid to read it.

It's what she wanted but I think you should read it alone. I'm going to go back to the car. She kissed him on the cheek and hugged him. When she walked back he looked out past the courts toward the path. The overhanging limbs had grown well over the opening and there was no way of knowing that it was once a space to walk through.

You are reading this letter because I am so overtaken by sadness and self-loathing that I do not feel I can go on anymore. You are reading this because my heart is broken, my dreams are lost and my time has come. I can no longer go on living with this pain inside. I am so alone and have not been able to find an escape.

I am so sorry mom and dad. You always did the best you could for me. I've let you down and I only wish I could have been a stronger person. My soul has been taken from me. The spirit I had as a child I can no longer remember.

David Mamet wrote that "Hope is what keeps us alive" but I no longer hope.

To my only true friend Brad I am sorry that you had to be a part of my life. The times we spent together were so special to me. What you did for me was good. I love you.

There are incidents that have happened in my life that were completely out of my control and that is not fair. It is not fair that I had to go through this. There was a time when I could not keep a smile from my face. I am now so filled with anger and have not been able to rid myself of it.

So let me go for now. Keep me close in your heart and mind. I will always be with you and you will always be with me as I move on.

Love, Kelly

THE END

*If you - or someone you know - are having thoughts
about suicide, call 1.800.SUICIDE (784-2433).
Calls are connected to a certified crisis center nearest
the caller's location. Services are available 24 hours a
day, seven days a week.*

National Sexual Assault Hotline
· 1.800.656.HOPE ·
Free. Confidential. 24/7.

Acknowledgements

The State Museum of Pennsylvania
Building the Suburban Dream

The Covenant House
Five Penn Plaza
New York NY 10001

The Pennsylvania Turnpike Commision
7631 Derry Street
Harrisburg, PA 17111

Daniel H. Pink, author of *Free Agent Nation: The Future of Working for Yourself* (Warner Business Books, 2002)

For more information or to join our online community, go to:

www.TheCourtsBook.com

www.ingramcontent.com/pod-product-compliance
Lightning Source LLC
Chambersburg PA
CBHW020817260626
47169CB00003B/706